THE RED HORIZON

THE RED HORIZON

BY

PATRICK MACGILL

WITH A FOREWORD BY
VISCOUNT ESHER G.C.B.

BRANDON

This Edition Published by
Brandon Book Publishers Limited,
Dingle, Co. Kerry, Ireland
1984

ISBN 0 86322 071 1

Printed and bound in Great Britain by Mackays of Chatham

TO

THE LONDON IRISH

TO THE SPIRIT OF THOSE WHO FIGHT AND TO THE MEMORY OF THOSE WHO HAVE PASSED AWAY THIS BOOK IS DEDICATED

FOREWORD

To Patrick MacGill,

Rifleman No. 3008, London Irish.

Dear Patrick MacGill,

There is open in France a wonderful exhibition of the work of the many gallant artists who have been serving in the French trenches through the long months of the War.

There is not a young writer, painter, or sculptor of French blood, who is not risking his life for his country. Can we make the same proud boast?

When I recruited you into the London Irish—one of those splendid regiments that London has sent to Sir John French, himself an Irishman—it was with gratitude and pride.

You had much to give us. The rare experiences of your boyhood, your talents, your brilliant hopes for the future. Upon all these the Western hills and loughs of your native Donegal seemed to have a prior claim. But you gave them to London and to our London Territorials. It was an example and a symbol.

The London Irish will be proud of their young artist in words, and he will for ever be proud of the London Irish Regiment, its deeds and valour, to which he has dedicated such great gifts. May God preserve you.

Yours sincerely,

ESHER.

President County of London

Callander. Territorial Association.

16th September, 1915.

CONTENTS

THE RED HORIZON

CHAPTER I

The Passing of the Regiment

I wish the sea were not so wide
That parts me from my love;
I wish the things men do below
Were known to God above.

I wish that I were back again
In the glens of Donegal;
They'll call me coward if I return,
But a hero if I fall.

"Is it better to be a living coward,
Or thrice a hero dead?"
"It's better to go to sleep, my lad,"
The Colour Sergeant said.

NIGHT, a grey troubled sky without moon or stars. The shadows lay on the surface of the sea, and the waves moaned beneath the keel of the troopship that was bearing us away on the most momentous journey of our lives. The hour was about ten. Southampton lay astern; by dawn we should be in France, and a day nearer the war for which we had trained so long in the cathedral city of St. Albans.

I had never realized my mission as a rifleman so acutely before.

"To the war! to the war!" I said under my breath. "Out to France and the fighting!" The thought raised a certain expectancy in my mind. "Did I think three years ago that I should ever be a soldier?" I asked myself. "Now that I am, can I kill a man; run a bayonet through his body; right through, so that the point, blood red and cruelly keen, comes out at the back? I'll not think of it."

But the thoughts could not be chased away. The month was March, and the night was bitterly cold on deck. A sharp penetrating wind swept across the sea and sung eerily about the dun-coloured funnel. With my overcoat buttoned well up about my neck and my Balaclava helmet pulled down over my ears I paced along the deck for quite an hour; then, shivering with cold, I made my way down to the cabin where my mates had taken up their quarters. The cabin was low-roofed and lit with two electric lamps. The corners receded into darkness where the shadows clustered thickly. The floor was covered with sawdust, packs and haversacks hung from pegs in the walls; a gun-rack stood in the centre of the apartment;

butts down and muzzles in line, the rifles stretched in a straight row from stern to cabin stairs. On the benches along the sides the men took their seats, each man under his equipment, and by right of equipment holding the place for the length of the voyage.

My mates were smoking, and the whole place was dim with tobacco smoke. In the thick haze a man three yards away was invisible.

"Yes," said a red-haired sergeant, with a thick blunt nose and a broken row of tobacco-stained teeth; "we're off for the doin's now."

"Blurry near time too," said a Cockney named Spud Higgles. "I thought we weren't goin' out at all."

"You'll be there soon enough, my boy," said the sergeant. "It's not all fun, I'm tellin' you, out yonder. I have a brother——"

"The same bruvver?" asked Spud Higgles.

"What d'ye mean?" inquired the sergeant.

"Ye're always speakin' about that bruvver of yours," said Spud. "'E's only in Ally Sloper's Cavalry; no man's ever killed in that mob."

"H'm!" snorted the sergeant. "The A.S.C. runs twice as much risk as a line regiment."

" That's why ye didn't join it then, is it?" asked the Cockney.

" Hold yer beastly tongue ! " said the sergeant.

" Well, it's like this," said Spud——

" Hold your tongue," snapped the sergeant, and Spud relapsed into silence.

After a moment he turned to me where I sat. " It's not only Germans that I'll look for in the trenches," he said, " when I have my rifle loaded and get close to that sergeant——"

" You'll put a bullet through him " ; I said, " just as you vowed you'd do to me some time ago. You were going to put a bullet through the sergeant-major, the company cook, the sanitary inspector, the army tailor and every single man in the regiment. Are you going to destroy the London Irish root and branch ? " I asked.

" Well, there's some in it as wants a talking to at times," said Spud. " 'Ave yer got a fag to spare ? "

Somebody sung a ragtime song, and the cabin took up the chorus. The boys bound for the fields of war were light-hearted and gay. A journey from the Bank to Charing Cross might be undertaken with a more serious air ; it looked for all the world as if they were merely out on some night frolic, determined to throw the whole mad vitality of youth into the escapade.

"What will it be like out there?" I asked myself. The war seemed very near now. "What will it be like, but above all, how shall I conduct myself in the trenches? Maybe I shall be afraid—cowardly. But no! If I can't bear the discomforts and terrors which thousands endure daily I'm not much good. But I'll be all right. Vanity will carry me through where courage fails. It would be such a grand thing to become conspicuous by personal daring. Suppose the men were wavering in an attack, and then I rushed out in front and shouted: 'Boys, we've got to get this job through'—But, I'm a fool. Anyhow I'll lie on the floor and have a sleep."

Most of the men were now in a deep slumber. Despite an order against smoking, given a quarter of an hour before, a few of my mates had the "fags" lit, and as the lamps had been turned off the cigarettes glowed red through the gloom. The sleepers lay in every conceivable position, some with faces turned upwards, jaws hanging loosely and tongues stretching over the lower lips; some with knees curled up and heads bent, frozen stiff in the midst of a grotesque movement, some with hands clasped tightly over their breasts and others with their fingers bent as if trying to clutch at something beyond their reach. A few slumbered with their heads on their rifles, more had their heads on the sawdust-covered floor, and these sent the sawdust fluttering whenever they breathed. The atmosphere of the place was close and almost suffocating. Now and again someone coughed and spluttered as if he were going to choke. Perspiration stood out in little beads on the temples of the sleepers, and they turned round from time to time to raise their Balaclava helmets higher over their eyes.

And so the night wore on. What did they dream of lying there? I wondered. Of their journey and the perils that lay before them? Of the glory or the horror of the war? Of their friends whom, perhaps, they would never see again? It was impossible to tell.

For myself I tried not to think too clearly of what I might see to-morrow or the day after. The hour was now past midnight and a new day had come. What did it hold for us all? Nobody knew—I fell asleep.

CHAPTER II

Somewhere in France

When I come back to England,
  And times of Peace come round,
I'll surely have a shilling,
  And may be have a pound;
I'll walk the whole town over,
  And who shall say me nay,
For I'm a British soldier
  With a British soldier's pay.

THE Rest Camp a city of innumerable bell-tents, stood on the summit of a hill overlooking the town and the sea beyond. We marched up from the quay in the early morning, followed the winding road paved with treacherous cobbles that glory in tripping unwary feet, and sweated to the summit of the hill. Here a new world opened to our eyes: a canvas city, the mushroom growth of our warring times lay before us; tent after tent, large and small, bell-tent and marquee in accurate alignment.

It took us two hours to march to our places; we grounded arms at the word of command and sank on our packs wearily happy. True, a few had fallen out; they came in as we rested and awkwardly fell into position. They were men who had been sea-sick the night before. We were too excited to rest for long; like dogs in a new locality we were presently nosing round looking for food. Two hours march in full marching order makes men hungry, and hungry men are ardent explorers. The dry and wet canteens faced one another, and each was capable of accommodating a hundred men. Never were canteens crowded so quickly, never have hundreds of the hungry and drouthy clamoured so eagerly for admission as on that day. But time worked marvels; at the end of an hour we fell in again outside a vast amount of victuals, and the sea-sickness of the previous night, and the strain of the morning's march were things over which now we could be humorously reminiscent.

Sheepskin jackets, the winter uniform of the trenches, were served out to us, and all were tried on. They smelt of something chemical and unpleasant, but were very warm and quite polar in appearance.

"Wish my mother could see me now," Bill the Cockney remarked. "My, she wouldn't think me 'alf a cove. It's a balmy. I discovered the South Pole, I'm thinkin'."

"More like you're up the pole!" some one cut in, then continued, "If they saw us at St. Albans* now! Bet yer they wouldn't say as we're for home service."

That night we slept in bell-tents, fourteen men in each, packed tight as herrings in a barrel, our feet festooning the base of the central pole, our heads against the lower rim of the canvas covering. Movement was almost an impossibility; a leg drawn tight in a cramp disturbed the whole fabric of slumbering humanity; the man who turned round came in for a shower of maledictions. In short, fourteen men lying down in a bell-tent cannot agree for very long, and a bell-tent is not a paradise of sympathy and mutual agreement.

We rose early, washed and shaved, and found our way to the canteen, a big marquee under the control of the Expeditionary Force, where bread and butter, bacon and tea were served out for breakfast. Soldiers recovering from wounds worked as waiters, and told, when they had a moment to spare, of hair-breadth adventures

* It was at St. Albans that we underwent most of our training.

in the trenches. They found us willing listeners; they had lived for long in the locality for which we were bound, and the whole raw regiment had a personal interest in the narratives of the wounded men. Bayonet-charges were discussed.

"I've been in three of 'em," remarked a quiet, inoffensive-looking youth who was sweeping the floor of the room. "They were a bit 'ot, but nothin' much to write 'ome about. Not like a picture in the papers, none of them wasn't. Not much stickin' of men. You just ops out of your trench and rush and roar, like 'ell. The Germans fire and then run off, and it's all over."

After breakfast feet were inspected by the medical officer. We sat down on our packs in the parade ground, took off our boots, and shivered with cold. The day was raw, the wind sharp and penetrating; we forgot that our sheepskins smelt vilely, and snuggled into them, glad of their warmth. The M.O. asked questions: "Do your boots pinch?" "Any blisters?" "Do you wear two pairs of socks?" &c., &c. Two thousand feet passed muster, and boots were put on again.

The quartermaster's stores claimed our attention afterwards, and the attendants there were almost uncannily kind. "Are you sure you've got everything you want?" they asked us. "There mayn't be a chance to get fitted up after this." Socks, pull-throughs, overcoats, regimental buttons, badges, hats, tunics, oil-bottles, gloves, puttees, and laces littered the floor and were piled on the benches. We took what we required; no one superintended our selection.

At St. Albans, where we had been turned into soldiers, we often stood for hours waiting until the quartermaster chose to give us a few inches of rifle-rag; here a full uniform could be obtained by picking it up. And our men were wise in selecting only necessities; they still remembered the march of the day before. All took sparingly and chose wisely. Fancy socks were passed by in silence, the homely woollen article, however, was in great demand. Bond Street was forgotten. The "nut" was a being of a past age, or, if he still existed, he was undergoing a complete transformation. Also he knew what socks were best for the trenches.

At noon we were again ready to set out on our journey. A tin of bully-beef and six biscuits, hard as rocks, were given to each man prior to departure. Sheepskins were rolled into shape and fastened on the tops of our packs, and with this additional burden on the shoulder we set out from the rest-camp and took our course down the hill. On the way we met another regiment coming up to fill our place, to sleep in our bell-tents, pick from the socks which we had left behind, and to meet for once, the first and last time perhaps, a quarter-master who is really kind in the discharge of his professional duties. We marched off, and sang our way into the town and station. Our trucks were already waiting, an endless number they seemed lined up in the siding with an engine in front and rear, and the notice "Hommes 40 chevaux 20" in white letters on every door. The night before I had slept in a bell-tent where a man's head pointed to each seam in the canvas, to-night it seemed as if I should sleep, if that were possible, in a still more crowded place, where we had now barely standing room, and where it was difficult to move about. But a much-desired relief came before the train started, spare waggons were shunted on, and a number of men were taken from each compartment and given room elsewhere. In fact, when we moved off we had only twenty-two soldiers in our place, quite enough though when our equipment, pack, rifle, bayonet, haversack, overcoat, and sheepskin tunic were taken into account.

A bale of hay bound with wire was given to us for bedding, and bully-beef, slightly flavoured, and biscuits were doled out for rations. Some of us bought oranges, which were very dear, and paid three halfpence apiece for them ; chocolate was also obtained, and one or two adventurous spirits stole out to the street, contrary to orders, and bought *café au lait* and *pain et beurre,* drank the first in the *estaminet,* and came back to their trucks munching the latter.

At noon we started out on the journey to the trenches, a gay party that found expression for its young vitality in song. The sliding-doors and the windows were open ; those of us who were not looking out of the one were looking out of the other. To most it was a new country, a place far away in peace and a favourite resort of the wealthy ; but now a country that called for any man, no matter how poor, if he were strong in person and willing to give his life away when called upon to do so. In fact, the poor man was having his first holiday on the

Continent, and alas!—perhaps his last; and like cattle new to the pasture fields in Spring, we were surging full of life and animal gaiety.

We were out on a great adventure, full of thrill and excitement; the curtain which surrounded our private life was being lifted; we stood on the threshold of momentous events. The cottagers who laboured by their humble homes stood for a moment and watched our train go by; now and again a woman shouted out a blessing on our mission, and ancient men seated by their doorsteps pointed in the direction our train was going, and drew lean, skinny hands across their throats, and yelled advice and imprecations in hoarse voices. We understood. The ancient warriors ordered us to cut the Kaiser's throat and envied us the job.

The day wore on, the evening fell dark and stormy. A cold wind from somewhere swept in through chinks in windows and door, and chilled the compartment. The favourite song, *Uncle Joe*, with its catching chorus,

> When Uncle Joe plays a rag upon his old banjo,
> Eberybody starts aswayin to and fro,
> Mummy waddles all around the cabin floor,
> Yellin' "Uncle Joe, give us more! give us more!"

died away into a melancholy whimper. Sometimes one of the men would rise, open the window and look out at a passing hamlet, where lights glimmered in the houses and heavy waggons lumbered along the uneven streets, whistle an air into the darkness and close the window again. My mate had an electric torch—by its light we opened the biscuit box handed in when we left the station, and biscuits and bully-beef served to make a rather comfortless supper. At ten o'clock, when the torch refused to burn, and when we found ourselves short of matches, we undid the bale, spread out the hay on the floor of the truck and lay down, wearing our sheepskin tunics and placing our overcoats over our legs.

We must have been asleep for some time. We were awakened by the stopping of the train and the sound of many voices outside. The door was opened and we looked out. An officer was hurrying by, shouting loudly, calling on us to come out. On a level space bordering the line a dozen or more fires were blazing merrily, and dixies with some boiling liquid were being carried backwards and forwards. A sergeant with a lantern, one of our own men, came to our truck and clambered inside.

"Every man get his mess tin," he shouted. "Hurry up, the train's not stopping for long, and there's coffee and rum for us all."

"I wish they'd let us sleep," someone who was fumbling in his pack remarked in a sleepy voice. "I'm not wantin' no rum and cawfee. Last night almost choked in the bell-tent, the night before sea-sick, and now wakened up for rum and cawfee. Blast it, I say!"

We lined up two deep on the six-foot way, shivering in the bitter cold, our mess-tins in our hands. The fires by the railway threw a dim light on the scene, officers paraded up and down issuing orders, everybody seemed very excited, and nearly all were grumbling at being awakened from their beds in the horse-trucks. Many of our mates were now coming back with mess-tins steaming hot, and some would come to a halt for a moment and sip from their rum and coffee. Chilled to the bone we drew nearer to the coffee dixies. What a warm drink it would be! I counted the men in front—there were no more than twelve or thirteen before me. Ah! how cold! and hot coffee—suddenly a whistle was blown, then another.

"Back to your places!" the order came, and never did a more unwilling party go back to bed. We did not learn the reason for the order ; in the army few explanations are made. We shivered and slumbered till dawn, and rose to greet a cheerless day that offered us biscuits and bully-beef for breakfast and bully-beef and biscuits for dinner. At half-past four in the afternoon we came to a village and formed into column of route outside the railway station. Two hours march lay before us we learned, but we did not know where we were bound. As we waited ready to move off a sound, ominous and threatening, rumbled in from the distance and quivered by our ears. We were hearing the sound of guns !

CHAPTER III

Our French Billets

The fog is white on Glenties moors,
The road is grey from Glenties town,
Oh ! lone grey road and ghost-white fog,
And ah ! the homely moors of brown.

THE farmhouse where we were billeted reminded me strongly of my home in Donegal with its fields and dusky evenings and its spirit of brooding quiet. Nothing will persuade me, except perhaps the Censor, that it is not the home of Marie Claire, it so fits in with the description in her book.

The farmhouse stands about a hundred yards away from the main road, with a cart track, slushy and muddy running across the fields to the very door. The whole aspect of the place is forbidding, it looks squalid and dilapidated, and smells of decaying vegetable matter, of manure and every other filth that can find a resting place in the vicinity of an unclean dwelling-place. But it is not dirty ; its home-made bread and beer are excellent, the new-laid eggs are delightful for breakfast, the milk and butter, fresh and pure, are dainties that an epicure might rave about.

We easily became accustomed to the discomforts of the place, to the midden in the centre of the yard, to the lean long-eared pigs that try to gobble up everything that comes within their reach, to the hens that flutter over our beds and shake the dust of ages from the barn-roof at dawn, to the noisy little children with the dirty faces and meddling fingers, who poke their hands into our haversacks, to the farm servants who inspect all our belongings when we are out on parade, and even now we have become accustomed to the very rats that scurry through the barn at midnight and gnaw at our equipment and devour our rations when they get hold of them. One night a rat bit a man's nose—but the tale is a long one and I will tell it at some other time.

We came to the farm forty of us in all, at the heel of a cold March day. We had marched far in full pack with rifle and bayonet. An additional load had now been heaped on our shoulders in the shape of the sheepskin jackets, the uniform of the trenches, indispensable to the firing line, but the last straw on the backs of overburdened soldiers. The march to the barn billet was a miracle of endurance, but all lived it through and thanked Heaven heartily when it was over. That night we slept in the barn, curled up in the straw, our waterproof sheets under us and our blankets and sheepskins round our bodies. It was very comfortable, a night, indeed, when one might wish to remain awake to feel how very glorious the rest of a weary man can be.

Awaking with dawn was another pleasure; the barn was full of the scent of corn and hay and of the cow-shed beneath. The hens had already flown to the yard and the dovecot was voluble. Somewhere near a girl was milking, and we could hear the lilt of her song as she worked; a cart rumbled off into the distance, a bell was chiming, and the dogs of many farms were exchanging greetings. The morning was one to be remembered.

But mixed with all these medley of sounds came one that was almost new; we heard it for the first time the day previous and it had been in our ears ever since; it was with us still and will be for many a day to come. Most of us had never heard the sound before, never heard its summons, its murmur or its menace. All night long it was in the air, and sweeping round the barn where we lay, telling all who chanced to listen that out there, where the searchlights quivered across the face of heaven, men were fighting and killing one another: soldiers of many lands, of England, Ireland and Scotland, of Australia, and Germany; of Canada, South Africa, and New Zealand; Saxon, Gurkha, and Prussian, Englishman, Irishman, and Scotchman were engaged in deadly combat. The sound was the sound of guns—our farmhouse was within the range of the big artillery.

We were billeted a platoon to a barn, a section to a granary, and despite the presence of rats and incidentally, pigs, we were happy. On one farm there were two pigs, intelligent looking animals with roguish eyes and queer rakish ears. They were terribly lean, almost as lean as some I have seen in Spain where the swine are as skinny as Granada beggars. They were very hungry and one ate a man's food-wallet and all it contained, comprising bread, army biscuits, canned beef, including can and other sundries. "I wish the animal had choked itself," my mate said when he discovered his loss. Personally I had a profound respect for any pig who voluntarily eats army biscuit.

We got up about six o'clock every morning and proceeded to wash and shave. All used the one pump, sometimes five or six heads were stuck under it at the same moment, and an eager hand worked the handle, and poured a plentiful supply of very cold water on the close cropped pates. The panes of the farmhouse window made excellent shaving mirrors and, incidentally, I may mention that rifle-slings generally serve the purpose of razor strops. Breakfast followed toilet; most of the men bought *café-au-lait*, at a penny a basin, and home-made bread, buttered lavishly, at a penny a slice. A similar repast would cost sixpence in London.

Parade then followed. In England we had cherished the illusion that life abroad would be an easy business, merely consisting of firing practices in the trenches, followed by intervals of idleness in rest-camps, where cigarettes could be obtained for the asking, and tots of rum would be served out *ad infinitum*. This rum would have a certain charm of its own, make everybody merry, and banish all discomforts due to frost and cold for ever. Thus the men thought, though most of our fellows are teetotallers. We get rum now, few drink it; we are sated with cigarettes, and smoke them as if in duty bound; the stolen delight of the last "fag-end" is a dream of the past. Parades are endless, we have never worked so hard since we joined the army; the minor offences of the cathedral city are full-grown crimes under long artillery range; a dirty rifle was only a matter for words of censure a month ago, a dirty rifle now will cause its owner to meditate in the guard-room.

Dinner consists of bully beef and biscuits; now and again we fry the bully beef on the farm-house stove, and when cash is plentiful cook an egg with it. The afternoon is generally given up to practising bayonet-fighting, and our day's work comes to an end about six o'clock. In the evening we go into the nearest village and discuss matters of interest in some *café*. Here we meet all manner of men, Gurkhas fresh from the firing line; bus-drivers, exiles from London; men of the Army Service Corps; Engineers, kilted Highlanders, men recovering from wounds, who are almost fit to go to the trenches again; French soldiers, Canadian soldiers, and all sorts of people, helpers in some way or another of the Allies in the Great War.

We have to get back to our billets by eight o'clock, to stop out after that hour is a serious crime here. A soldier out of doors at midnight in the cathedral city was merely a minor offender. But under the range of long artillery fire all things are different for the soldier.

St. Patrick's Day was an event. We had a half holiday, and at night, with the aid of beer, we made merry as men can on St. Patrick's Day. We sang Irish songs, told stories, mostly Cockney, and laughed without restraint as merry men will, for to all St. Patrick was an admirable excuse for having a good and rousing time.

There is, however, one little backwater of rest and quiet into which we men of blood and iron drift at all too infrequent intervals—that is when we become what is known officially as "barn orderly." A barn orderly is the company unit who looks after the billets of the men out on parade. In due course my turn arrived, and the battalion marched away leaving me to the quiet of farmyard.

Having heaped up the straw, our bedding, in one corner of the barn, swept the concrete floor, rolled the blankets, explained to the gossipy farm servant that I did not "compree" her gibberish, and watched her waddle across the midden towards the house, my duties were ended. I was at liberty until the return of the battalion. It was all very quiet, little was to be heard save the gnawing of the rats in the corner of the barn and the muffled booming of guns from "out there"—"out there" is the oft repeated phrase that denotes the locality of the firing line.

There was sunlight and shade in the farm-yard, the sun lit up the pump on the top of which a little bird with salmon-pink breast, white-tipped tail, and crimson head preened its feathers ; in the shade where our barn and the stables form an angle an old lady in snowy sunbonnet and striped apron was sitting knitting. It was good to be there lying prone upon the barn straw near the door above the crazy ladder, writing letters. I had learned to love this place and these people whom I seem to know so very well from having read René Bazin, Daudet, Maupassant, Balzac and Marie Claire. High up and far away to the west a Zeppelin was to be seen travelling in a westerly direction ; the farmer's wife, our landlady, had just rescued a tin of bully beef from one of her all-devouring pigs ; at the barn door lay my recently cleaned rifle and ordered equipment—how incongruous it all was with the home of Marie Claire.

Suddenly I was brought back to realities by the recollection that the battalion was to have a bath that afternoon and towels and soap must be ready to take out on the next parade.

The next morning was beautifully clear; the sun rising over the firing line lit up wood and field, river and pond. The hens were noisy in the farmyard, the horse lines to the rear were full of movement, horses strained at their tethers eager to break away and get free from the captivity of the rope; the grooms were busy brushing the animals' legs and flanks, and a slight dust arose into the air as the work was carried on.

Over the red-brick houses of the village the church stood high, its spire clearly defined against the blue of the sky. The door of the *café* across the road opened, and the proprietress, a merry-faced, elderly woman, came across to the farmhouse. She purchased some newly laid eggs for breakfast, and entered into conversation with our men, some of whom knew a little of her language. They asked about her son in the trenches; she had heard from him the day before and he was quite well and hoped to have a holiday very soon. He would come home then and spend a fortnight with the family. She looked forward to his coming, he had been away from her ever since the war started; she had not seen him for eight whole months. What happiness would be hers when he returned! She waved her hand to us as she went off, tripping lightly across the roadway and disappearing into the *café*. She was going to church presently; it was Holy Week when the Virgin listened to special intercessors, and the good matron of the *café* prayed hourly for the safety of her soldier boy.

At ten o'clock we went to chapel, our pipers playing *The Wearing of the Green* as we marched along the crooked village streets, our rifles on our shoulders and our bandoliers heavy with the ball cartridge which we carried. The rifle is with us always now, on parade, on march, in *café*, billet, and church; our "best friend" is our eternal companion. We carried it into the church and fastened the sling to the chair as we knelt in prayer before the altar. We occupied the larger part of the building, only three able-bodied men in civilian clothing were in attendance.

The youth of the country were out in the trenches, and even here in the quiet little chapel with its crucifixes, images, and pictures, there was the suggestion of war in the collection boxes for wounded soldiers, in the crêpe worn by so many women ; one in every ten was in mourning, and above all in the general air of resignation which showed on all the faces of the native worshippers.

The whole place breathed war, not in the splendid whirlwind rush of men mad in the wild enthusiasm of battle, but in silent yearning, heartfelt sorrow, and great bravery, the bravery of women who remain at home. Opposite us sat the lady of the *café*, her head low down on her breast, and the rosary slipping bead by bead through her fingers. Now and again she would stir slightly, raise her eyes to the Virgin on the right of the high altar, and move her lips in prayer, then she would lower her head again and continue her rosary.

As far as I could ascertain singing in church was the sole privilege of the choir, none of the congregation joined in the hymns. But to-day the church had a new congregation—the soldiers from England, the men who sing in the trenches, in the billet, and on the march ; the men who glory in song on the last lap of a long, killing journey in full marching order. To-day they sang a hymn well-known and loved, the clarion call of their faith was started by the choir. As one man the soldiers joined in the singing, and their voices filled the building. The other members of the congregation looked on for a moment in surprise, then one after another they started to sing, and in a moment nearly all in the place were aiding the choir. One was silent, however, the lady of the *café*; still deep in prayer she scarcely glanced at the singers, her mind was full of another matter. Only a mother thinking about a loved son can so wholly lose herself from the world. And as I looked at her I thought I detected tears in her eyes.

The priest, a pleasant faced young man, who spoke very quickly (I have never heard anybody speak like him), thanked the soldiers, and through them their nation for all that was being done to help in the war; prayers were said for the men at the front, those who were still alive, as well as those who had given up their lives for their country's sake, and before leaving we sang the national anthem, our's, *God Save the King*.

With the pipers playing at our front, and an

admiring crowd of boys following, we took our way back to our billets. On the march a mate was speaking, one who had been late coming on parade in the morning.

"Saw the woman of the *café* in church?" he asked me. "Saw her crying?"

"I thought she looked unhappy."

"Just after you got off parade the news came," my mate told me. "Her son had been killed. She is awfully upset about it and no wonder. She was always talking about her *petit garçon*, and he was to be home on holidays shortly."

Somewhere "out there" where the guns are incessantly booming, a nameless grave holds the "*petit garçon*," the *café* lady's son; next Sunday another mourner will join with the many in the village church and pray to the Virgin Mother for the soul of her beloved boy.

CHAPTER IV

The Night Before the Trenches

Four by four in column of route,
By roads that the poplars sentinel,
Clank of rifle and crunch of boot—
All are marching and all is well.
White, so white is the distant moon,
Salmon-pink is the furnace glare,
And we hum, as we march, a ragtime tune,
Khaki boys in the long platoon,
Going and going—anywhere.

THE battalion will move to-morrow," said the Jersey youth, repeating the orders read out in the early part of the day, and removing a clot of farmyard muck from the foresight guard of his rifle as he spoke. It was seven o'clock in the evening, the hour when candles were stuck in their cheese sconces and lighted. Cakes of soap and lumps of cheese are easily scooped out with clasp-knives and make excellent sconces; we often use them for that purpose in our barn billet. We had been quite a long time in the place and had grown to like it. But to-morrow we were leaving.

"Oh, dash the rifle!" said the Jersey boy, getting to his feet and kicking a bundle of straw across the floor of the barn. "To-morrow night we'll be in the trenches up in the firing line."

"The slaughter line," somebody remarked in the corner where the darkness hung heavy. A match was lighted disclosing the speaker's face and the pipe which he held between his teeth.

"No smoking," yelled a corporal, who had just entered. "You'll burn the damned place down and get yourself as well as all of us into trouble."

"Oh blast the barn!" muttered Bill Sykes, a narrow chested Cockney with a good-humoured face that belied his nickname. "It's only fit for rats and there's 'nuff of 'em 'ere. I'm goin' to 'ave a fag anyway. Got me?"

The corporal asked Bill for a cigarette and lit it. "We're all mates now and we'll make a night of it," he cried. "Damn the barn, there'll be barns when we're all washed out with Jack Johnsons. What are you doin', Feelan?"

Feelan, an Irishman with a brogue that could be cut with a knife, laid down the sword which he was burnishing and glanced at the non-com.

"The Germans don't fire at men with stripes, I hear," he remarked, "They only shoot rale good soldiers. A livin' corp'ral's hardly as good as a dead rifleman."

Six foot three of Cumberland bone and muscle detached itself from the straw and looked round the barn. We call it Goliath on account of its size.

" Who's to sing the first song," asked Goliath. " A good hearty song ! "

" One with whiskers on it ! " said the corporal.

" I'll slash the game up and give a rale ould song, whiskers to the toes of it," said Feelan, shoving his sword in its scabbard and throwin himself flat back on the straw. " Its a song about the time Irelan' was fightin' for freedom and it's called *The Rising of the Moon !* A great song entirely it is, and I cannot do it justice."

Feelan stood up, his legs wide apart and both his thumbs stuck in the upper pockets of his tunic. Behind him the barn stretched out into the gloom that our solitary candle could not pierce. On either side rifles hung from the wall, and packs and haversacks stood high from the straw in which most of the men had buried themselves, leaving nothing but their faces, fringed with the rims of Balaclava helmets, exposed to view. The night was bitterly cold, outside where the sky stood high splashed with countless stars and where the earth gripped tight on itself, the frost fiend was busy; in the barn, with its medley of men, roosting hens and prowling rats all was cosy and warm. Feelan cleared his throat and commenced the song, his voice strong and clear filled the barn:—

"Arrah! tell me Shan O'Farrel; tell me why you hurry so?"
"Hush, my bouchal, hush and listen," and his cheeks were all aglow—
"I've got orders from the Captain to get ready quick and soon
For the pikes must be together at the risin' of the moon,
At the risin' of the moon!
At the risin' of the moon!
And the pikes must be together at the risin' of the moon!"

"That's some song," said the corporal. "It has got guts in it. I'm sick of these ragtime rotters!"

"The old songs are always the best ones," said Feelan, clearing his throat preparatory to commencing a second verse.

"What about *Uncle Joe?*" asked Goliath, and was off with a regimental favourite.

When Uncle Joe plays a rag upon his old banjo—
("Oh!" the occupants of the barn yelled.)
Ev'rybody starts a swayin' to and fro—
("Ha!" exclaimed the barn.)
Mummy waddles all around the cabin floor!—
("What!" we chorused.)
Crying, "Uncle Joe, give us more, give us more!"

" Give us no more of that muck ! " exclaimed Feelan, burrowing into the straw, no doubt a little annoyed at being interrupted in his song. " Damn ragtime ! "

" There's ginger in it ! " said Goliath. " Your old song is as flat as French beer ! "

" Some decent music is what you want," said Bill Sykes, and forthwith began strumming an invisible banjo and humming *Way down upon the Swanee Ribber.*

The candle, the only one in our possession, burned closer to the cheese sconce, a daring rat slipped into the light, stopped still for a moment on top of a sheaf of straw, then scampered off again, shadows danced on the roof, over the joists where the hens were roosting, an unsheathed sword glittered brightly as the light caught it, and Feelan lifted the weapon and glanced at it.

" Burnished like a lady's nail," he muttered.

" Thumb nail ? " interrogated Goliath.

" Ragnail, p'raps," said the Cockney.

" I wonder whether we'll have much bayonet-fightin' or not ? " remarked the Jersey boy looking at each of us in turn and addressing no one in particular.

" We'll get some now and again to keep us

warm ! " said the corporal. " It'll be 'ot when it comes along."

" 'Ot's not the word," said Bill ; " I never was much drawn to soldierin' 'fore the war started, but when it came along I felt I'd like to 'ave a 'and in the gime. There, that candle's goin' out ! "

" Bunk ! " roared the corporal, putting his pipe in his pocket and seizing a blanket, the first to hand. Almost immediately he was under the straw with the blanket wrapped round him. We were not backward in following, and all were in bed when the flame which followed the wax so greedily died for lack of sustenance.

To-morrow night we should be in the trenches.

CHAPTER V

First Blood

The nations like Kilkenny cats,
Full of hate that never dies out,
Tied tail to tail, hung o'er a rope,
Still strive to tear each other's eyes out.

THE company came to a halt in the village; we marched for three miles, and the morning being a hot one we were glad to fall out and lie down on the pavement, packs well up under our shoulders and our legs stretched out at full length over the kerbstone into the gutter. The sweat stood out in beads on the men's foreheads and trickled down their cheeks on to their tunics. The white dust of the roadway settled on boots, trousers, and putties, and rested in fine layers on haversack folds and cartridge pouches. Rifles and bayonets, spotless in the morning's inspection, had lost all their polished lustre and were gritty to the touch. We carried a heavy load, two hundred rounds of ball cartridge, a loaded rifle with five rounds in magazine, a pack stocked with overcoat, spare underclothing, and other field necessaries, a haversack containing twenty-four hours rations, and sword and entrenching tool per man. We were equipped for battle and were on our way towards the firing line.

A low-set man with massive shoulders, bull-neck and heavy jowl had just come out of an *estaminet,* a mess-tin of beer in his hand, and knife and fork stuck in his putties.

"Going up to the slaughter line, mateys?" he enquired, an amused smile hovering about his eyes, which took us all in with one penetrating glance.

"Yes," I replied. "Have you been long out here?"

"About a matter of nine months."

"You've been lucky," said Mervin, my mate.

"I haven't gone West yet, if that's what you mean," was the answer. "'Oo are you?"

"The London Irish."

"Territorials?"

"That's us," someone said.

"First time up this way?"

"First time."

"I knew that by the size of your packs," said the man, the smile reaching his lips. "Bloomin' pack-horses you look like. If you want a word of advice, sling your packs over a hedge, keep a tight grip of your mess-tin, and ram your spoon and fork into your putties. My pack went West at Mons."

" You were there then ? "

" Blimey, yes." was the answer.

" How did you like it ? "

" Not so bad," said the man. " 'Ave a drink and pass the mess-tin round. There is only one bad shell, that's the one that 'its you, and if you're unlucky it'll come your way. The same about the bullet with your number on it ; it can't miss you if it's made for you. And if ever you go into a charge—Think of your pals, matey ! " he roared at the man who was greedily gulping down the contents of the messtin, " You're swigging all the stuff yourself. For myself I don't care much for this beer, it has no guts in it, one good English pint is worth an ocean of this dashed muck. Good-bye "—we were moving off, " and good luck to you ! "

Mervin, perspiring profusely, marched by my side. He and I have been great comrades, we have worked, eaten, and slept together, and committed sin in common against regimental regulations. Mervin has been a great traveller, he has dug for gold in the Yukon, grown oranges in Los Angeles, tapped for rubber in Camerango

(I don't know where the place is, but I love the name), and he can eat a tin of bully beef, and relish the meal. He is the only man in our section who can enjoy it, one of us cares only for cheese, and few grind biscuits when they can beg bread.

A battalion is divided into four companies, a company contains four platoons made up of sections of unequal strength; our section consisted of thirteen—there are only four boys left now, Mervin has been killed, five have been wounded, two have become stretcher bearers, and one has left us to join another company in which one of his mates is placed. Poor Mervin! How sad it was to lose him, and much sadder is it for his sweetheart in England. He was engaged; often he told me of his dreams of a farm, a quiet cottage and a garden at home when the war came to an end. Somewhere in a soldier's grave he sleeps. I know not where he lies, but one day, if the fates spare me, I will pay a visit to the resting-place of a true comrade and a staunch friend.

Outside the village we formed into single file. It was reported that the enemy shelled the road daily, and only three days before the Royal Engineers lost thirty-seven men when going up to the trenches on the same route.

In the village all was quiet, the *cafés* were open, and old men, women, and boys were about their daily work as usual. There were very few young men of military age in the place ; all were engaged in the business of war.

A file marched on each side of the road. Mervin was in front of me ; Stoner, a slender youth, tall as a lance and lithe as a poplar, marched behind, smoking a cigarette and humming a tune. He worked as a clerk in a large London club whose members were both influential and wealthy. When he joined the army all his pay was stopped, and up to the present he has received from his employers six bars of chocolate and four old magazines. His age is nineteen, and his job is being kept open for him. He is one of the cheeriest souls alive, a great worker, and he loves to listen to the stories which now and again I tell to the section. When at St. Albans he spent six weeks in hospital suffering from tonsilitis. The doctor advised him to stay at home and get his discharge ; he is still with us, and once, during our heaviest bombardment, he slept for a whole eight hours in his dug-out. All the rest of us remained awake, feeling certain that our last hour had come.

Teak and Kore, two bosom chums, marched on the other side of the road. Both are children almost; they may be nineteen, but neither look it; Kore laughs deep down in his throat, and laughs heartiest when his own jokes amuse the listeners. He is not fashioned in a strong mould, but is an elegant marcher, and light of limb; he may be a clerk in business, but as he is naturally secretive we know nothing of his profession. Kore is also a punster who makes abominable puns; these amuse nobody except, perhaps, himself. Teak, a good fellow, is known to us as Bill Sykes. He has a very pale complexion, and has the most delightful nose in all the world; it is like a little white potato. Bill is a good-humored Cockney, and is eternally involved in argument. He carries a Jew's harp and a mouth-organ, and when not fingering one he is blowing music-hall tunes out of the other.

Goliath, six foot three of bone and muscle, is a magnificent animal. The gods forgot little of their old-time cunning in the making of him, in the forging of his shoulders, massive as a bull's withers, in the shaping of his limbs, sturdy as pillars of granite and supple as willows, in the setting of his well-poised head, his heavy jaw, and muscled neck. But the gods seem to have grown weary of a momentous masterpiece when they came to the man's eyes, and Goliath wears glasses. For all that he is a good marksman and, strange to say, he delights in the trivialities of verse, and carries an ear-marked Tennyson about with him.

Pryor is a pessimist, an artist, a poet, a writer of stories; he drifted into our little world on the march and is with us still. He did not like his previous section and applied for a transfer into ours. He gloats over sunsets, colours, unconventional doings, hopes that he will never marry a girl with thick ankles, and is certain that he will never live to see the end of the War. Pryor, Teak, Kore, and Stoner have never used a razor; they are as beardless as babes.

We were coming near the trenches. In front, the two lines of men stretched on as far as the eye could see; we were near the rear and singing *Macnamara's Band,* a favourite song with our regiment. Suddenly a halt was called. A heap of stones bounded the roadway, and we sat down, laying our rifles on the fine gravel.

The crash came from the distance, probably five hundred yards in front, and it sounded like a waggon-load of rubble being emptied on a landing and clattering down a flight of stairs.

"What's that?" asked Stoner, flicking the ash from the tip of his cigarette with the little finger.

"Some transport has broken down."

"Perhaps it's a shell," I ventured, not believing what I said.

"Oh! your grandmother."

Whistling over our head it came with a swish similar to that made by a wet sheet shaken in the wind, and burst in the field on the other side of the road. A ball of white smoke poised for a moment in mid-air, curled slowly upwards, and gradually faded away. I looked at my mates. Stoner was deadly pale; it seemed as if all the blood had rushed away from his face. Teak's mouth was a little open, his cigarette, sticking to his upper lip, hung down quivering, and the ash was falling on his tunic; a smile almost of contempt played on Pryor's face, and Goliath yawned. At the time I wondered if he were posing. He spoke:—

"There's only one bad shell, you know," he said. "It hasn't come this way yet. See that woman?" He pointed at the field where the shell had exploded. At the far end a woman was working with a hoe, her head bowed over her work, and her back bent almost double. Two children, a boy and a girl, came along the road hand in hand, and deep in a childish discussion. The world, the fighting men, and the bursting shells were lost to them. They were intent on their own little affairs. For ourselves we felt more than anything else a sensation of surprise—surprise because we were not more afraid of the bursting shrapnel.

"Quick march!"

We got to our feet and resumed our journey. We were now passing through a village where several houses had been shattered, and one was almost levelled to the ground. But beside it, almost intact, although not a pane of glass remained in the windows, stood a *café*. A pale stick of a woman in a white apron, with arms akimbo, stood on the threshold with a toddling infant tugging at her petticoats.

Several French soldiers were inside, seated round a table, drinking beer and smoking. One man, a tall, angular fellow with a heavy beard, seemed to be telling a funny story; all his mates were laughing heartily. A horseman came up at this moment, one of our soldiers, and his horse was bleeding at the rump, where a red, ugly gash showed on the flesh.

"Just a splinter of shell," he said, in answer to our queries. "The one that burst there," he pointed with his whip towards the field where the shrapnel had exploded: "'Twas only a whistler."

"What did you think of it," I called to Stoner.

"I didn't know what to think first," was the answer, "then when I came to myself I thought it might have done for me, and I got a kind of shock just like I'd get when I have a narrow shave with a 'bus in London."

"And you, Pryor?"

"I went cold all over for a minute."

"Bill?"

"Oh! Blast them is what I say!" was his answer. "If it's going to do you in 'twill do you in, and that's about the end of it. Well, sing a song to cheer us up," and without another word he began to bellow out one of our popular rhymes.

> Oh! the Irish boys they are the boys
> To drive the Kaiser balmy.
> And *we'll* smash up that fool Von Kluck
> And all his bloomin' army!

We came to a halt again, this time alongside

a Red Cross motor ambulance. In front, with the driver, one of our boys was seated ; his coat sleeve ripped from the shoulder, and blood trickling down his arm on to his clothes ; inside, on the seat, was another with his right leg bare and a red gash showing above the knee. He looked dazed, but was smoking a cigarette.

"Stopped a packet, matey ?" Stoner enquired.

"Got a scratch, but it's not worth while talking about," was the answer. "I'll remember you to your English friends when I get back."

"You're all right, matey," said a regular soldier who stood on the pavement, addressing the wounded man. "I'd give five pounds for a wound like that. You're damned lucky, and its your first journey !"

"Have you been long out here ?" asked Teak.

"Only about nine months," replied the regular. "There are seven of the old regiment left, and it makes me wish this damned business was over and done with."

"Ye don't like war, then."

"Like it ! Who likes it ? only them that's miles away from the stinks, and cold, and heat, and everything connected with the —— work."

"But this is a holy war," said Pryor, an inscrutable smile playing round his lips. "God's with us, you know."

"We're placing more reliance on gunpowder than on God," I remarked.

"Blimey! talk about God!" said the regular. "There's more of the damned devil in this than there is of anything else. They take us out of the trenches for a rest, send us to church, and tell us to love our neighbours. Blimey! next day they send you up to the trenches again and tell you to kill like 'ell."

"Have you ever been in a bayonet charge?" asked Stoner.

"Four of them," we were told, "and I don't like the blasted work, never could stomach it."

The ambulance waggon whirred off, and the march was resumed.

We were now about a mile from the enemy's lines, and well into the province of death and desolation. We passed the last ploughman. He was a mute, impotent figure, a being in rags, guiding his share, and turning up little strips of earth on his furrowed world. The old home, now a jumble of old bricks getting gradually hidden by the green grasses, the old farm holed by a thousand shells, the old plough, and the old horses held him in bondage. There was no other world for the man; he was a dumb worker, crawling along at the rear of the destructive demon War, repairing, as far as he was able, the damage which had been done.

We came to a village, literally buried. Holes dug by high explosive shells in the roadway were filled up with fallen masonry. This was a point at which the transports stopped. Beyond this, man was the beast of burden—the thing that with scissors-like precision cut off, pace by pace, the distance between him and the trenches. There is something pathetic in the forward crawl, in the automatic motion of boots rising and falling at the same moment; the gleaming sword handles waving backwards and forwards over the hip, and, above all, in the stretcher-bearers with stretchers slung over their shoulders marching along in rear. The march to battle breathes of something of an inevitable event, of forces moving towards a destined end. All individuality is lost, the thinking ego is effaced, the men are spokes in a mighty wheel, one moving because the other must, all fearing death as hearty men fear it, and all bent towards the same goal.

We were marched to a red brick building with a shrapnel-shivered roof, and picks and shovels were handed out to us.

"You've got to help to widen the communication trench to-day!" we were told by an R.E. officer who had taken charge of our platoon.

As we were about to start a sound made quite familiar to me what time I was in England as a marker at our rifle butts, cut through the air, and at the same moment one of the stray dogs which haunt their old and now unfamiliar localities like ghosts, yelled in anguish as he was sniffing the gutter, and dropped limply to the pavement. A French soldier who stood in a near doorway pulled the cigarette from his bearded lips, pointed it at the dead animal, and laughed. A comrade who was with him shrugged his shoulders deprecatingly.

"That dashed sniper again!" said the R.E. officer.

"Where is he?" somebody asked innocently.

"I wish we knew," said the officer. "He's behind our lines somewhere, and has been at this game for weeks. Keep clear of the roadway!" he cried, as another bullet swept through the air, and struck the wall over the head of the laughing Frenchman, who was busily rolling a fresh cigarette.

Four of our men stopped behind to bury the dog, the rest of us found our way into the communication trench. A signboard at the entrance, with the words "To Berlin," stated in trenchant words underneath, "This way to the war."

The communication trench, sloping down from the roadway, was a narrow cutting dug into the cold, glutinous earth, and at every fifty paces in alternate sides a manhole, capable of holding a soldier with full equipment, was hollowed out in the clay. In front shells were exploding, and now and again shrapnel bullets and casing splinters sung over our heads, for the most part delving into the field on either side, but sometimes they struck the parapets and dislodged a pile of earth and dust, which fell on the floor of the trench. The floor was paved with bricks, swept clean, and almost free from dirt; there was a general air of cleanliness about the place, the level floor, the smooth sides, and the well-formed parapets. An Engineer walking along the top, and well back from the side, counted us as we walked along in line with him. He had taken charge of our section as a working party, and when he turned to me in making up his tally I saw that he wore a ribbon on his breast.

" He has got the Distinguished Conduct Medal," Mervin whispered. " How did you get it ? " he called up to the man.

" Just the luck of war," was the modest answer. " Eleven, twelve, thirteen, that will be quite sufficient for me. Are you just new out ? " he asked.

" Oh, we've been a few weeks in training here."

We met another Engineer coming out, his face was dripping with blood, and he had a khaki handkerchief tied round his hand.

" How did it happen ? " I asked.

" Oh, a damned pip-squeak (a light shrapnel shell) caught me on the parapet," he laughed, squeezing into a manhole. " Two of your boys have copped it bad along there. No, I don't think it was your fellows. Who are you ? "

" The London Irish."

" Oh ! 'twasn't you, 'twas the ——," he said, rubbing a miry hand across the jaw, dripping with blood, " I think the two poor devils are done in. Oh, this isn't much," he continued, taking out a spare handkerchief and wiping his face, " 'twon't bring me back to England, worse luck ! Are you from Chelsea ? "

" Yes."

" What about the chances for the Cup Final ? " he asked, and somebody took up the thread of conversation as I edged on to the spot where the two men lay.

They were side by side, face upwards, in a disused trench that branched off from ours ; the hand of one lay across the arm of the other, and the legs of both were curled up to their knees, almost touching their chests. They were mere boys, clean of lip and chin and smooth of forehead, no wrinkles had ever traced a furrow there. One's hat was off, it lay on the floor under his head. A slight red spot showed on his throat, there was no trace of a wound. His mate's clothes were cut away across the belly, the shrapnel had entered there under the navel, and a little blood was oozing out on to the trouser's waist, and giving a darkish tint to the brown of the khaki. Two stretcher-bearers were standing by, feeling, if one could judge by the dejected look on their faces, impotent in the face of such a calamity. Two first field dressings, one open and the contents trod on the ground, the other fresh as when it left the hands of the makers, lay idle beside the dead man. A little distance to the rear a youngster was looking vacantly across the parapet, his eyes fixed on the ruined church in front, but his mind seemed to be deep in something else, a problem which he failed to solve.

One of the stretcher-bearers pointed at the youth, then at the hatless body in the trench.

" Brothers," he said.

For a moment a selfish feeling of satisfaction welled up in our lungs. Teak gave it expression, his teeth chattering even as he spoke, " It might be two of us, but it isn't," and somehow with the thought came a sensation of fear. It might be our turn next, as we might go under to-day or to-morrow; who could tell when the turn of the next would come? And all that day I was haunted by the figure of the youth who was staring so vacantly over the rim of the trench, heedless of the bursting shells and indifferent to his own safety.

The enemy shelled persistently. Their objective was the ruined church, but most of their shells flew wide or went over their mark, and made matters lively in Harley Street, which ran behind the house of God.

" Why do they keep shellin' the church?"

Bill asked the engineer, who never left the parapet even when the shells were bursting barely a hundred yards away. Like the rest of us, Bill took the precaution to duck when he heard the sound of the explosion.

"That's what they always do," said Stoner, "I never believed it even when I read it in the papers at home, but now —"

"They think that we've ammunition stored there," said the engineer, "and they always keep potting at the place."

"But have we?"

"I dunno."

"We wouldn't do it," said Kore, who was of a rather religious turn of mind. "But they, the bounders, would do anything. Are they the brutes the papers make them out to be? Do they use dum-dum bullets?"

"This is war, and men do things that they'd not do in the ordinary way," was the non-committal answer of the Engineer.

"Have you seen many killed?" asked Mervin.

"Killed!" said the man on the parapet. "I think I have! You don't go through this and not see sights. I never even saw a dead man before this war. Now!" he paused. "That what we saw just now," he continued, alluding to the death of the two soldiers in the trench, "never moves me. *You'll* feel it a bit being just new out, but when you're a while in the trenches you'll get used to it."

In front a concussion shell blew in a part of the trench, filling it up to the parapet. That afternoon we cleared up the mess and put down a flooring of bricks in a newly opened corner. When night came we went back to the village in the rear. "The Town of the Last Woman" our men called it. Slept in cellars and cooked our food, our bully stew, our potatoes, and tea in the open. Shells came our way continually, but for four days we followed up our work and none of our battalion "stopped a packet."

CHAPTER VI

IN THE TRENCHES

Up for days in the trenches,
  Working and working away;
Eight days up in the trenches
  And back again to-day.
Working with pick and shovel,
  On traverse, banquette, and slope,
And now we are back and working
  With tooth-brush, razor, and soap.

WE had been at work since five o'clock in the morning, digging away at the new communication trench. It was nearly noon now, and rations had not come; the cook's waggons were delayed on the road.

Stoner, brisk as a bell all the morning, suddenly flung down his shovel.

"I'm as hungry as ninety-seven pigs," he said, and pulled a biscuit from his haversack. "Now I've got 'dog,' who has 'maggot'?"

"Dog and maggot" means biscuit and cheese, but none of us had the latter; cheese was generally flung into the incinerator, where it wasted away in smoke and smell. This happened of course when we were new to the grind of war.

"I've found out something," said Mervin, rubbing the sweat from his forehead and looking over the parapet towards the firing line. A shell whizzed by, and he ducked quickly. We all laughed, the trenches have got a humour peculiarly their own.

"There's a house in front," said Mervin, "where they sell *café noir* and *pain et beurre*."

"Git," muttered Bill. "Blimey, there's no one 'ere but fools like ourselves."

"I've just been in the house," said Mervin, who had really been absent for quite half an hour previously. "There are two women there, a mother and daughter. A good-looking girl, Bill." The eyes of the Cockney brightened.

"Twopence a cup for black coffee, and the same for bread and butter."

"No civilians are allowed here," Pryor remarked.

"It's their own home," said Mervin. "They've never left the place, and the roof is broken and half the walls blown away."

"I'm for coffee," Stoner cried, jumping over the parapet and stopping a shower of muck which a bursting shell flung in his face. We were with him immediately, and presently found ourselves at the door of a red brick cottage with all the windows smashed, roof riddled with shot, and walls broken, just as Mervin had described.

A number of our men were already inside feeding. An elderly, well-dressed woman, with close-set eyes, rather thick lips, and a short nose, was grinding coffee near a flaming stove, on which an urn of boiling water was bubbling merrily. A young girl, not at all good-looking but very sweet in manner, said "Bonjour, messieurs," as we entered, and approached each of us in turn to enquire into our needs. Mervin knew the language, and we placed the business in his hands, and sat down on the floor paved with red bricks; the few chairs in the house were already occupied.

The house was more or less in a state of disorder; the few pictures on the wall, the portrait of the woman herself, *The Holy Family Journeying to Egypt*, a print of Millet's *Angelus*, and a rude etching of a dog hung anyhow, the frames smashed and the glass broken. A Dutch clock, with figures of nymphs on the face, and the timing piece of a shell dangling from the weights, looked idly down, its pendulum gone and the glass broken.

Bill, naughty rascal that he is, wanted a kiss with his coffee, and finding that Mervin refused to explain this to the girl, he undertook the matter himself.

"Madham mosselle," he said, lingering over every syllable, "I get no milk with cawfee, compree?" The girl shook her head, but seemed to be amused.

"Not compree," he continued, "and me learnin' the lingo. I don't like French, you spell it one way and speak it the other. Nark (confound) it, I say, Mad-ham-moss-elle, voo (what's "give," Mervin?) dunno, that's it. Voo dunno me a kiss with the cawfee, compree, it's better'n milk."

"Don't be a pig, Bill," Stoner cut in. "It's not fair to carry on like that."

"Nark you, Stoner!" Bill answered. "It mayn't be fair, but it'd be nice if I got one."

"Kiss a face like yours," muttered Mervin, "she'd have a taste for queer things if she did."

"There's no accountin' for tastes, you know," said Bill. "Oh, Blimey, that's done it," he cried, stooping low as a shell exploded overhead, and drove a number of bullets into the roof. The old woman raised her head for a moment and crossed herself, then she continued her work; the daughter looked at Bill, laughed, and punched him on the shoulder. In the action there was a certain contempt, and Bill forthwith relapsed into silence and troubled the girl no further. When we got out to our work again he spoke.

"She was a fine hefty wench," he said, "I'm tip over toes in love with her."

"She's not one that I'd fancy," said Stoner.

"Her finger nails are so blunt," mumbled Pryor, "I never could stand a woman with blunt finger nails."

"What is your ideal of a perfect woman, Pryor?" I asked.

"There is no perfect woman," was his answer, "none that comes up to my ideal of beauty. Has she a fair brow? It's merely a space for wrinkles. Are her eyes bright? What years of horror when you watch them grow watery and weak with age. Are her teeth pearly white? The toothache grips them and wears them down to black and yellow stumps. Is her body graceful, her waist slender, her figure upright. She becomes a mother, and every line of her person is distorted, she becomes a nightmare to you. Ah, perfect woman! They could not tashion you in Eden! When I think of a woman washing herself! Ugh! Your divinity washes the dust from her hair and particles of boiled beef from between her teeth! Think of it, Horatio!"

"Nark it, you fool," said Bill, lifting a fag end from the bottom of the trench and lighting it at mine. "Blimey, you're balmy as nineteen maggots!"

It was a few days after this incident that, in the course of a talk with Stoner, the subject of trenches cropped up.

"There are trenches and trenches," he remarked, as we were cutting poppies from the parapet and flinging the flowers to the superior slope. "There are some as I almost like, some as I don't like, and some so bad that I almost ran away from them."

For myself I dislike the narrow trench, the one in which the left side keeps fraying the cloth of your sleeve, and the right side strives to open furrows in your hand. You get a surfeit of damp, earthy smell in your nostrils, a choking sensation in your throat, for the place is suffocating. The narrow trench is the safest, and most of the English communication trenches are narrow—so narrow, indeed, that a man with a pack often gets held, and sticks there until his comrades pull him clear.

The communication trenches serve, however, for more purposes than for the passage of troops; during an attack the reserves wait there, packed tight as sardines in a tin. When a man lies down he lies on his mate, when he stands up, if he dare to do such a thing, he runs the risk of being blown to eternity by a shell. Rifles, packs, haversacks, bayonets, and men are all messed up in an intricate jumble, the reserves lie down like rats in a trap, with their noses to the damp earth, which always reminds me of the grave. For them there is not the mad exhilaration of the bayonet charge, and the relief of striking back at the aggressor. They lie in wait, helpless, unable to move backward or forward, ears greedy for the latest rumours from the active front, and hearts prone to feelings of depression and despair.

The man who is seized with cramp groans feebly, but no one can help him. To rise is to court death, as well as to displace a dozen grumbling mates who have inevitably become part of the human carpet that covers the floor of the trench. A leg moved disturbs the whole pattern; the sufferer can merely groan, suffer, and wait. When an attack is on the communication trenches are persistently shelled by the enemy with a view to stop the advance of reinforcements. Once our company lay in a trench as reserves for fourteen hours, and during that time upwards of two thousand shells were hurled in our direction, our trench being half filled with rubble and clay. Two mates, one on my right and one on my left, were wounded. I did not receive a scratch, and Stoner slept for eight whole hours during the cannonade ; but this is another story.

Before coming out here I formed an imaginary picture of the trenches, ours and the enemy's, running parallel from the Vosges in the South to the sea in the North. But what a difference I find in the reality. Where I write the trenches run in a strange, eccentric manner. At one point the lines are barely eighty yards apart ; the ground there is under water in the wet season ; the trench is built of sandbags ; all rifle fire is done from loopholes, for to look over the parapet is to court certain death. A mountain of coal-slack lies between the lines a little further along, which are in " dead " ground that cannot be covered by rifle fire, and are 1,200 yards apart. It is here that the sniper plies his trade. He hides somewhere in the slack, and pots at our men from dawn to dusk and from dusk to dawn. He knows the range of every yard of our communication trenches. As we come in we find a warning board stuck up where the parapet is crumbling away. "Stoop low, sniper," and we crouch along head bent until the danger zone is past.

Little mercy is shown to a captured sniper; a short shrift and swift shot is considered meet penalty for the man who coolly and coldly singles out men for destruction day by day. There was one, however, who was saved by Irish hospitality. An Irish Guardsman, cleaning his telescopic-rifle as he sat on the trench banquette, and smoking one of my cigarettes told me the story.

"The coal slack is festooned with devils of snipers, smart fellows that can shoot round a corner and blast your eye-tooth out at five hundred yards," he said. "They're not all their ones, neither; there's a good sprinkling of our own boys as well. I was doing a wee bit of pot-shot-and-be-damned-to-you work in the other side of the slack, and my eyes open all the time for an enemy's back. There was one near me, but I'm beggared if I could find him.

'I'll not lave this place till I do,' I says to meself, and spent half the nights I was there prowlin' round like a dog at a fair with my eyes open for the sniper. I came on his post wan night. I smelt him out because he didn't bury his sausage skins as we do, and they stunk like the hole of hell when an ould greasy sinner is a-fryin'. In I went to his sandbagged castle, with me gun on the cock and me finger on the trigger, but he wasn't there; there was nothin' in the place but a few rounds of ball an' a half empty bottle. I was dhry as a bone, and I had a sup without winkin'. 'Mother of Heaven,' I says, when I put down the bottle, 'its little ye know of hospitality, stranger, leaving a bottle with nothin' in it but water. I'll wait for ye, me bucko,' and I lay down in the corner and waited for him to come in.

"But sorrow the fut of him came, and me waiting there till the colour of day was in the sky. Then I goes back to me own place, and there was he waiting for me. He only made one mistake, he had fallen to sleep, and he just sprung up as I came in be the door.

"Immediately I had him by the big toe. 'Hands up, Hans'! I said, and he didn't argue, all that he did was to swear like one of ourselves and flop down. 'Why don't ye bury yer sausages, Hans ?' I asked him. 'I smelt yer, me bucko, by what ye couldn't eat. Why didn't ye have something better than water in yer bottle ?' I says to him. Dang a Christian word would he answer, only swear, an swear with nothin' bar the pull of me finger betwixt him and his Maker. But, ye know, I had a kind of likin' for him when I thought of him comin' in to my house without as much as yer leave, and going to sleep just as if he was in his own home. I didn't swear back at him but just said, 'This is only a house for wan, but our King has a big residence for ye, so come along before it gets any clearer,' and I took him over to our trenches as stand-to was coming to an end."

Referring again to our trenches there is one portion known to me where the lines are barely fifty yards apart, and at the present time the grass is hiding the enemy's trenches ; to peep over the parapet gives one the impression of looking on a beautiful meadow splashed with daisy, buttercup, and poppy flower ; the whole is a riot of colour—crimson, heliotrope, mauve, and green. What a change from some weeks ago ! Then the place was littered with dead bodies, and limp, lifeless figures hung on to the barbed wire where they had been caught in a mad rush to the trenches which they never took. A breeze blows across the meadow as I write, carrying with it the odour of death and perfumed flowers, of aromatic herbs and summer, of desolation and decay. It is good that Nature does her best to blot out all traces of the tragedy between the trenches.

There is a vacant spot in our lines, where there is no trench and none being constructed; why this should be I do not know. But all this ground is under machine-gun fire and within rifle range. No foe would dare to cross the open, and the foe who dared would never live to get through. Further to the right, is a pond with a dead German stuck there, head down, and legs up in air. They tell me that a concussion shell has struck him since and part of his body was blown over to our lines. At present the pond is hidden and the light and shade plays over the kindly grasses that circle round it. On the extreme right there is a graveyard. The trench is deep in dead men's bones and is considered unhealthy. A church almost razed to the ground, with the spire blown off and buried point down in the earth, moulders in ruins at the back. It is said that the ghosts of dead monks pray nightly at the shattered altar, and some of our men state that they often hear the organ playing when they stand as sentries on the banquette.

"The fire trench to-night," said Stoner that evening, a nervous light in his soft brown eyes, as he fumbled with the money on the card table. His luck had been good, and he had won over six francs; he generally loses. "Perhaps we're in for the high jump when we get up there."

"The high jump?" I queried, "what's that?"

"A bayonet charge," he replied, dealing a final hand and inviting us to double the stakes as the deal was the last. A few wanted to play for another quarter of an hour, but he would not prolong the game. Turning up an ace he shoved the money in his pocket and rose to his feet.

In an hour we were ready to move. We carried much weight in addition to our ordinary load, firewood, cooking utensils, and extra loaves. We bought the latter at a neighbouring *boulangerie*, one that still plied its usual trade in dangerous proximity to the firing-line.

The loaves cost $6\frac{1}{2}d.$ each, and we prefer them to the English bread which we get now and again, and place them far above the tooth-destroying army biscuits. Fires were permitted in the trenches, we were told, and our officers advised us to carry our own wood with us. So it came about that the enemy's firing served as a useful purpose; we pulled down the shrapnel shattered rafters of our billets, broke them up into splinters with our entrenching tools, and tied them up into handy portable bundles which we tied on our packs.

At midnight we entered Harley Street, and squeezed our way through the narrow trench. The distance to the firing-line was a long one; traverse and turning, turning and traverse, we thought we should never come to the end of them. There was no shelling, but the questing bullet was busy, it sung over our heads or snapped at the sandbags on the parapet, ever busy on the errand of death and keen on its mission. But deep down in the trench we regarded it with indifference. Our way was one of safety. Here the bullet was foiled, and pick and shovel reigned masters in the zone of death.

We were relieving the Scots Guards (many

of my Irish friends belong to this regiment). Awaiting our coming, they stood in the full marching order of the regulations, packs light, forks and spoons in their putties, and all little luxuries which we still dared to carry flung away. They had been holding the place for seven days, and were now going back somewhere for a rest.

" Is this the firing-line ? " asked Stoner.

" Yes, sonny," came the answer in a voice which seemed to be full of weariness.

" Quiet here ? " Mervin enquired, a note of awe in his voice.

" Naethin' doin'," said a fresh voice that reminded me forcibly of Glasgow and the Cowcaddens. " It's a gey soft job here."

" No casualties ? "

" Yin or twa stuck their heads o'er the parapet when they shouldn't and they copped it," said Glasgow, " but barrin' that 'twas quiet."

In the traverse where I was planted I dropped into Ireland; heaps of it. There was the brogue that could be cut with a knife, and the humour that survived Mons and the Marne, and the kindliness that sprang from the cabins of Corrymeela and the moors of Derrynane.

"Irish?" I asked.

"Sure," was the answer. "We're everywhere. Ye'll find us in a Gurkha regiment if you scratch the beggars' skins. Ye're not Irish!"

"I am," I answered.

"Then you've lost your brogue on the boat that took ye over," somebody said. "Are ye dry?"

I wiped the sweat from my forehead as I sat down on the banquette. "Is there something to drink?" I queried.

"There's a drop of cold tay, me boy," the man near me replied. "Where's yer mess-tin, Mike?"

A tin was handed to me, and I drank greedily of the cold black tea. The man Mike gave some useful hints on trench work.

"It's the Saxons that's across the road," he said, pointing to the enemy's lines which were very silent. I had not heard a bullet whistle over since I entered the trench. On the left was an interesting rifle and machine gun fire all the time. "They're quiet fellows, the Saxons, they don't want to fight any more than we do, so there's a kind of understanding between us. Don't fire at us and we'll not fire at you. There's a good dug-out there," he continued, pointing to a dark hole in the parados (the rear wall of the trench), " and ye'll find a pot of jam and half a loaf in the corner. There's also a water jar half full."

" Where do you get water ? "

" Nearly a mile away the pump is," he answered. " Ye've to cross the fields to get it."

" A safe road ? " asked Stoner.

" Not so bad, ye know," was the answer.

" This place smells 'orrid," muttered Bill, lighting a cigarette and flinging off his pack. " What is it ? "

" Some poor devils between the trenches ; they've been lyin' there since last Christmas."

" Blimey, what a stink," muttered Bill " Why don't ye bury them up ? "

" Because nobody dare go out there, me boy," was the answer. " Anyway, it's Germans they are. They made a charge and didn't get as far as here. They went out of step so to speak."

" Woo–oo–oo ! " Bill suddenly yelled and kicked a tin pail on to the floor of the trench. A shower of sparks flew up into the air and fluttered over the rim of the parapet. " I put my 'and on it, 'twas like a red 'ot poker, it burned me to the bone!"

"It's the brazier ye were foolin' about with," said Mike, who was buckling his pack-straps preparatory to moving, "See, and don't put yer head over the top, and don't light a fire at night. Ye can put up as much flare as you like by day. Good-bye, boys, and good luck t'ye."

"Any Donegal men in the battalion?" I called after him as he was moving off.

"None that I know of," he shouted back, "but there are two other battalions that are not here, maybe there are Donegal men there. Good luck, boys, good luck!"

We were alone and lonely, nearly every man of us. For myself I felt isolated from the whole world, alone in front of the little line of sand bags with my rifle in my hand. Who were we? Why were we there? Goliath, the junior clerk, who loved Tennyson; Pryor, the draughtsman, who doted on Omar; Kore, who read Fanny Eden's penny stories, and never disclosed his profession; Mervin, the traveller, educated for the Church but schooled in romance; Stoner, the clerk, who reads my books and says he never read better; and Bill, newsboy, street-arab, and Lord knows what, who reads *The Police News*, plays innumerable tricks with cards, and gambles and never wins. Why were we here holding a line of trench, and ready to take a life or give one as occasion required? Who shall give an answer to the question?

CHAPTER VII

BLOOD AND IRON—AND DEATH

At night the stars are shining bright,
  The old-world voice is whispering near,
We've heard it when the moon was light,
  And London's streets were verydear;
But dearer now they are, sweetheart,
  The 'buses running to the Strand,
But we're so far, so far apart,
  Each lonely in a different land.

THE night was murky and the air was splashed with rain. Following the line of trench I could dimly discern the figures of my mates pulling off their packs and fixing their bayonets. These glittered brightly as the dying fires from the trench braziers caught them, and the long array of polished blades shone into their place along the dark brown sandbags. Looking over the parados I could see the country in rear, dim in the hazy night. A white, nebulous fog lay on the ground and enveloped the lone trees that stood up behind. Here and there I could discern houses where no light shone, and where no people dwelt. All the inhabitants were gone, and in the village away to the right there was absolute silence, the stillness of the desert. To my mind came words I once read or heard spoken, "The conqueror turns the country into a desert, and calls it peace."

I clamped my bayonet into its standard and rested the cold steel on the parapet, the point showing over; and standing up I looked across to the enemy's ground.

"They're about three hundred yards away," somebody whispered taking his place at my side. "I think I can see their trenches."

An indistinct line which might have been a parapet of sandbags, became visible as I stared through the darkness; it looked very near, and my heart thrilled as I watched. Suddenly a stream of red sparks swooped upwards into the air and circled towards us. Involuntarily I stooped under cover, then raised my head again. High up in the air a bright flame stood motionless lighting up the ground in front, the space between the lines. Every object was visible: a tree stripped of all its branches stood bare, outlined in black; at its foot I could see the barbed wire entanglements, the wire sparkling as if burnished; further back was a ruined cottage, the bare beams and rafters giving it the appearance of a skeleton. A year ago a humble farmer might have lived there; his children perhaps played where dead were lying. I could see the German trench, the row of sandbags, the country to rear, a ruined village on a hill, the flashes of rifles on the left....the flare died out in mid-air and darkness cloaked the whole scene again.

"What do you think of it, Stoner?" I asked the figure by my side.

"My God, it's great," he answered. "To think that they're over there, and the poor fellows lying out on the field!"

"They're their own bloomin' tombstones, anyway," said Bill, cropping up from somewhere.

"I feel sorry for the poor beggars," I said.

"They'll feel sorry for themselves, the beggars," said Bill.

"There, what's that?"

It crept up like a long white arm from behind the German lines, and felt nervously at the clouds as if with a hand. Moving slowly from North to South it touched all the sky, seeking for something. Suddenly it flashed upon us, almost dazzling our eyes. In a flash Bill was upon the banquette.

" Nark the doin's, nark it," he cried and fired his rifle. The report died away in a hundred echoes as he slipped the empty cartridge from its breech.

" That's one for them," he muttered.

" What did you fire at ? " I asked.

" The blasted searchlight," he replied, rubbing his little potato of a nose. " That's one for 'em, another shot nearer the end of the war ! "

" Did you hit it ? " asked our corporal.

" I must 'ave 'it it, I fired straight at it."

" Splendid, splendid," said the corporal. " Its only about three miles away though."

" Oh, blimey ! . . . ."

Sentries were posted for the night, one hour on and two off for each man until dawn. I was sentry for the first hour. I had to keep a sharp look out if an enemy's working party showed itself when the rockets went up. I was to fire at it and kill as many men as possible. One thinks of things on sentry-go.

" How can I reconcile myself to this," I asked, shifting my rifle to get nearer the parapet. " Who are those men behind the line of sandbags that I should want to kill them, to disembowel them with my sword, blow their faces to pieces at three hundred yards, bomb them into eternity at a word of command. Who am I that I should do it; what have they done to me to incur my wrath? I am not angry with them; I know little of the race; they are utter strangers to me; what am I to think, why should I think?

"Bill," I called to the Cockney, who came by whistling, "what are you doing?"

"I'm havin' a bit of rooty (food) 'fore goin' to kip (sleep)."

"Hungry?

"'Ungry as an 'awk," he answered. "Give me a shake when your turn's up; I'm sentry after you."

There was a pause.

"Bill!"

"Pat?"

"Do you believe in God?"

"Well, I do and I don't," was the answer.

"What do you mean?"

"I don't 'old with the Christian business," he replied, "but I believe in God."

"Do you think that God can allow men to go killing one another like this?"

"Maybe 'E can't help it."

"And the war started because it had to be?

" It just came—like a war-baby."

Another pause.

" Yer write songs, don't yer ? " Bill suddenly asked.

" Sometimes."

" Would yer write me one, just a little one ? ' he continued. " There was a bird (girl) where I used to be billeted at St. Albans, and I would like to send 'er a bit of poetry."

" You've fallen in love ? " I ventured.

" No, not so bad as that —"

" You've not fallen in love."

" Well its like this," said my mate, " I used to be in 'er 'ouse and she made 'ome-made torfee."

" Made it well ? "

" Blimey, yes ; 'twas some stuff, and I used to get 'eaps of it. She used to slide down the banisters, too. Yer should 'ave seen it, Pat. It almost made me write poetry myself."

" I'll try and do something for you," I said. " Have you been in the dug-out yet ? "

" Yes, it's not such a bad place, but there's seven of us in it," said Bill, " it's 'ot as 'ell. But we wouldn't be so bad if Z— was out of it. I don't like the feller."

" Why ? " I asked, Z— was one of our thirteen, but he couldn't pull with us. For some reason or other we did not like him.

" Oh, I don't like 'im, that's all," was the answer. " Z— tries to get the best of everything. Give ye a drink from 'is water bottle when your own's empty ; 'e wouldn't. I wouldn't trust 'im that much." He clicked his thumb and middle finger together as he spoke, and without another word he vanished into the dug-out.

On the whole the members of our section, divergent as the poles in civil life, agree very well. But the same does not hold good in the whole regiment ; the public school clique and the board school clique live each in a separate world, and the line of demarcation between them is sharply drawn. We all live in similar dug-outs, but we bring a new atmosphere into them. In one, full of the odour of Turkish cigarettes, the spoken English is above suspicion ; in another, stinking of regimental shag, slang plays skittles with our language. Only in No. 3 is there two worlds blent in one ; our platoon officer says that we are a most remarkable section, consisting of literary men and babies.

"Stand-to!"

I rose to my feet, rubbing the sleep from my eyes, and promptly hit my head a resounding blow on the roof. The impact caused me to take a pace forward, and my boot rested on Stoner's face.

"Get out of it, you clumsy Irish beggar!" he yelled, jumping up and stumbling over Mervin, who was presently afoot and marching over another prostrate form.

"Stand-to! Stand-to!"

We shuffled out into the open, and took up our posts on the banquette, each in fighting array, equipped with 150 rounds of ball cartridge and entrenching tool handle on hip. In the trenches we always sleep in our equipment, by day we wear our bayonets in scabbard, at night the bayonets are always fixed.

"Where's Z—?" asked Stoner, as we stood to our rifles.

"In the dug-out," I told him, "he's asleep."

"'E is, is 'e?" yelled Bill, rushing to the door. "Come out of it lazybones," he called. "Show a leg at once, and grease to your gun. The Germans are on the top of us. Come out and get shot in the open."

Z— stumbled from his bed and blinked at us as he came out.

"Is it true, Bill, are they 'ere?" he asked.

"If they were 'ere you'd be a lot of good, you would," said Bill. "Get on with the work."

In the dusk and dawning we stand-to in the trenches ready to receive the enemy if he attempt to charge. Probably on the other side he waits for our coming. Each stand-to lasts for an hour, but once in a fog we stood for half a day.

The dawn crept slowly up the sky, the firing on the left redoubled in intensity, but we could not now see the flashes from the rifles. The last star-rocket rose from the enemy's trench, hung bright in mid-air for a space, and faded away. The stretch of ground between the trenches opened up to our eyes. The ruined cottage, cold and shattered, standing mid-way, looked lonely and forbidding. Here and there on the field I could see grey, inert objects sinking down, as it were, on the grass.

"I suppose that's the dead, the things lying on the ground," said Stoner. "They must be cold poor devils, I almost feel sorry for them."

The birds were singing, a blackbird hopped on to the parapet, looked enquiringly in, his yellow bill moving from side to side, and fluttered away; a lark rose into the heavens warbling for some minutes, a black little spot on the grey clouds; he sang, then sank to earth again, finding a resting place amongst the dead. We could see the German trenches distinctly now, and could almost count the sandbags on the parapet. Presently on my right a rifle spoke. Bill was firing again.

"Nark the doin's, Bill, nark it," Goliath shouted, mimicking the Cockney accent. "You'll annoy those good people across the way."

"An if I do!"

"They may fire at you!" said monumental Goliath with fine irony.

"Then 'ere's another," Bill replied, and fired again.

"Don't expose yourself over the parapet," said our officer, going his rounds. "Fire through the loop-holes if you see anything to fire at, but don't waste ammunition."

The loop-holes, drilled in steel plates wedged in the sandbags, opened on the enemy's lines; a hundred yards of this front was covered by each rifle; we had one loop-hole in every six yards, and by day every sixth man was posted as sentry.

Stoner, diligent worker that he is, set about preparing breakfast when stand-to was over. In an open space at the rear of the dug-out he fixed his brazier, chopped some wood, and soon had the regimental issue of coke ablaze.

"I'll cut the bacon," I said, producing the meat which I had carried with me.

"Put the stuff down here," said Stoner, "and clear out of it."

Stoner, busy on a job, brooks no argument, he always wants to do the work himself. I stood aside and watched. Suddenly an object, about the size of a fat sausage, spun like a big, lazy bee through the air, and fifty paces to rear, behind a little knoll, it dropped quietly, as if selecting a spot to rest on.

"It's a bird," said Stoner, "one without wings."

It exploded with terrific force, and blew the top of the knoll into the air; a shower of dust swept over our heads, and part of it dropped into Stoner's fire.

"That's done it," he exclaimed, "what the devil was it?"

No explanation was forthcoming, but later we discovered that it was a bomb, one of the morning greetings that now and again come to us from the German trench mortars. This was the first we had seen ; some of our fellows have since been killed by them ; and the blue-eyed Jersey youth who was my friend at St. Albans, and who has been often spoken of in my little volume *The Amateur Army*, came face to face with one in the trenches one afternoon. It had just been flung in, and, accompanied by a mate, my friend rounded a traverse in a deserted trench and saw it lying peacefully on the floor.

" What is it ? " he asked, coming to a halt.

" I don't know, it looks like a bomb ! " was the sudden answering yell. " Run."

A dug-out was near, and both shoved in, the Jersey boy last. But the bomb was too quick for him. Half an hour later the stretcher-bearers carried him out, wounded in seventeen places.

Stoner's breakfast was a grand success. The tea was admirable and the bacon, fried in the mess-tin lids, was done to a turn. In the matter of food we generally fare well, for our boys get a great amount of eatables from home, also they have money to spend, and buy most of their food whenever that is possible.

In the forenoon Pryor and I took up two earthen jars, a number of which are supplied to the trenches, and went out with the intention of getting water. We had a long distance to go, and part of the way we had to move through the trenches, then we had to take the road branching off to the rear. The journey was by no means a cheery one ; added to the sense of suffocation, which I find peculiar to the narrow trench, were the eternal soldiers' graves. At every turn where the parados opened to the rear they stared you in the face, the damp, clammy, black mounds of clay with white crosses over them. Always the story was the same ; the rude inscription told of the same tragedy : a soldier had been killed in action on a certain date. He might have been an officer, otherwise he was a private, a being with a name and number ; now lying cold and silent by the trench in which he died fighting. His mates had placed little bunches of flowers on his grave. Then his regiment moved off and the flowers faded. In some cases the man's cap was left on the black earth, where the little blades of kindly grass were now covering it up.

Most of the trench-dwellers were up and about, a few were cooking late breakfasts, and some were washing. Contrary to orders, they had stripped to the waist as they bent over their little mess-tins of soapy water; all the boys seemed familiar with trench routine. They were deep in argument at the door of one dug-out, and almost came to blows. The row was about rations. A light-limbed youth, with sloping shoulders, had thrown a loaf away when coming up to the trenches. He said his pack was heavy enough without the bread. His mates were very angry with him.

"Throwin' the grub away!" one of them said. "Blimey, to do a thing like that! Get out, Spud 'Iggles!"

"Why didn't yer carry the rooty yourself?"

"Would one of us not carry it?"

"Would yer! Why didn't ye take it then?"

"Why didn't ye give it to us?"

"Blimey, listen to yer jor!" said Spud Higgles, the youth with the sloping shoulders. "Clear out of it, nuff said, ye brainless twisters!"

"I've more brains than you have," said one of the accusers who, stripped to the waist, was washing himself.

"'Ave yer? so 'ave I," was the answer of the boy who lost the loaf, as he raised a mess-tin of tea from the brazier.

"Leave down that mess-tin for a minute and I'll show yer who has the most brains," said the man who was washing, sweeping the soapsuds from his eyes and bouncing into an aggressive attitude, with clenched fists before him, in true fighting manner.

"Leave down my mess-tin then!" was the answer. "Catch me! I've lost things that way before, I'ave."

Spud Higgles came off victor through his apt sarcasm. The sarcastic remark tickled the listeners, and they laughed the aggressive soldier into silence.

A number of men were asleep, the dug-outs were crowded, and a few lay on the banquette, their legs stretched out on the sand-bag platforms, their arms hanging loosely over the side, and their heads shrouded in Balaclava helmets. At every loop-hole a sentry stood in silent watch, his eyes rivetted on the sandbags ahead. Now and again a shot was fired, and sometimes, a soldier enthusiastic in a novel position, fired several rounds rapid across No-man's land into the enemy's lines, but much to the man's discomfiture no reply came from the other side.

"Firin' at beastly sandbags!" one of the

men said to me, " Blimey, that's no game. Yer 'ere and the sandbags is there, you never see anything, and you've to fire at nothin'. They call this war. Strike me ginger if it's like the pictures in *The Daily* —— ; them papers is great liars ! "

" Do you want to kill men ? " I asked.

" What am I here for ? " was the rejoinder. " If I don't kill them they'll kill me.'

No trench is straight at any place ; the straight line is done away with in the make-up of a trench. The traverse, jutting out in a sharp angle to the rear, gives way in turn to the fire position, curving towards the enemy, and there is never more than twelve yards liable to be covered by enfilade fire. The traverse is the home of spare ammunition, of ball cartridge, bombs, and hand-grenades. These are stored in depots dug into the wall of the trench. There are two things which find a place anywhere and everywhere, the biscuit and the bully beef. Tins of both are heaped in the trenches ; sometimes they are used for building dug-outs and filling revetements. Bully beef and biscuits are seldom eaten ; goodness knows why we are supplied with them.

We came into the territory of another battalion, and were met by an officer.

" Where are you going ? " he asked.

" For water, sir," said Pryor.

" Have you got permission from your captain ? "

" No, sir."

" Then you cannot get by here without it. It's a Brigade order," said the officer. " One of our men got shot through the head yesterday when going for water."

" Killed, sir," I enquired.

" Killed on the spot," was the answer.

On our way back we encountered our captain superintending some digging operation.

" Have you got the water already ? " he asked.

" No, sir."

" How is that ? "

" An officer of the —— wouldn't let us go by without a written permission."

" Why ? "

" He said it was a Brigade order," was Pryor's naïve reply. He wanted to go up that perilous road. The captain sat down on a sandbag, took out a slip of paper (or borrowed one from Pryor), placed his hat on his knee and the paper on his hat, and wrote us out the pass.

For twenty yards from the trench the road was sheltered by our parapet, past that lay the beaten zone, the ground under the enemy's rifle fire. He occupied a knoll on the left, the spot where the fighting was heavy on the night before, and from there he had a good view of the road. We hurried along, the jars striking against our legs at every step. The water was obtained from a pump at the back of a ruined villa in a desolate village. The shrapnel shivered house was named Dead Cow Cottage. The dead cow still lay in the open garden, its belly swollen and its left legs sticking up in the air like props in an upturned barrel. It smelt abominably, but nobody dared go out into the open to bury it.

The pump was known as Cock Robin Pump. A pencilled notice told that a robin was killed by a Jack Johnson near the spot on a certain date. Having filled our jars, Pryor and I made a tour of inspection of the place.

In a green field to the rear we discovered a graveyard, fenced in except at our end, where a newly open grave yawned up at us as if aweary of waiting for its prey.

"Room for extension here," said Pryor. "I suppose they'll not close in this until the graves reach the edge of the roadway. Let's read the epitaphs."

How peaceful the place was. On the right I could see through a space between the walls of the cottage the wide winding street of the village, the houses, cornstacks, and the waving bushes, and my soul felt strangely quieted. In its peace, in its cessation from labour, there was neither anxiety nor sadness, there remained rest, placid and sad. It seemed as if the houses, all intact at this particular spot, held something sacred and restful, that with them and in them all was good. They knew no evil or sorrow. There was peace, the desired consummation of all things—peace brought about by war, the peace of the desert, and death.

I looked at the first grave, its cross, and the rude lettering. This was the epitaph; this and nothing more:—

"An Unknown British Soldier."

On a grave adjoining was a cheap gilt vase with flowers, English flowers, faded and dying. I looked at the cross. One of the Coldstream Guards lay there killed in action six weeks before. I turned up the black-edged envelope on the vase, and read the badly spelt message, "From his broken-hearted wife and loving little son Tommy."

We gazed at it for a moment in silence. Then Pryor spoke. "I think we'll go back," he said, and there was a strained note in his voice; it seemed as if he wanted to hide something.

On our way out to the road we stopped for a moment and gazed through the shattered window of Dead Cow Cottage. The room into which we looked was neatly furnished. A round table with a flower vase on it stood on the floor, a number of chairs in their proper position were near the wall, a clock and two photos, one of an elderly man with a heavy beard, the other of a frail, delicate woman, were on the mantlepiece. The pendulum of the clock hung idle; it must have ceased going for quite a long time. As if to heighten a picture of absolute comfort a cat sat on the floor washing itself.

"Where will the people be?" I asked.

"I don't know," answered Pryor. "Those chairs will be useful in our dug-out. Shall we take them?"

We took one apiece, and with chair on our

head and jar in hand we walked towards the trenches. The sun was out, and it was now very hot. We sweated. My face became like a wet sponge squeezed in the hand; Pryor's face was very red.

"We'll have a rest," he said, and laying down the jar he placed his chair in the road and sat on it. I did the same.

"You know Omar?" he asked.

"In my calf-age I doated on him," I answered.

"What's the calf-age?"

"The sentimental period that most young fellows go through," I said. "They then make sonnets to the moon, become pessimistic, criticise everything, and feel certain that they will become the hub of the universe one day. They prefer vegetable food to pork, and read Omar."

"Have you come through the calf-age?"

"Years ago! You'll come through, too, Pryor —"

A bullet struck the leg of my chair and carried away a splinter of wood. I got to my feet hurriedly. "Those trenches seem quite a distance away," I said, hoisting my chair and gripping the jar as I moved off, "and we'll be safer when we're there."

All the way along we were sniped at, but we managed to get back safely. Finding that our supply of coke ran out we used the chairs for firewood.

CHAPTER VIII

TERRORS OF THE NIGHT

Buzz fly and gad fly, dragon fly and blue,
When you're in the trenches come and visit you,
They revel in your butter-dish and riot on your ham,
Drill upon the army cheese and loot the army jam.
They're with you in the dusk and the dawning and the noon,
They come in close formation, in column and platoon.
There's never zest like Tommy's zest when these have got to die:
For Tommy takes his puttees off and straffs the blooming fly.

"SOME are afraid of one thing, and some are afraid of another," said Stoner, perching himself on the banquette and looking through the periscope at the enemy's lines. "For myself I don't like shells—especially when in the open, even if they are bursting half a mile away."

"Is that what you fear most?" I asked.

"No, the rifle bullet is a thing I dread; the saucy little beggar is always on the go."

"What do you fear most, Goliath?" I asked the massive soldier who was cleaning his bayonet with a strip of emery cloth.

"Bombs," said the giant, "especially the

one I met in the trench when I was going round the traverse. It lay on the floor in front of me. I hardly knew what it was at first, but a kind of instinct told me to stand and gaze at it. The Germans had just flung it into the trench and there it lay, the bounder, making up its mind to explode. It was looking at me, I could see its eyes — "

"Git out," said Bill, who was one of the party.

"Of course, you couldn't see the thing's eyes," said Goliath, "you lack imagination. But I saw its eyes, and the left one was winking at me. I almost turned to jelly with fear, and Lord knows how I got back round the corner. I did, however, and then the bomb went bang! 'Twas some bang that, I often hear it in my sleep yet."

"We'll never hear the end of that blurry bomb," said Bill. "For my own part I am more afraid of —— "

"What?"

"—— the sergeant-major than anythink in this world or in the next!"

I have been thrilled with fear three times since I came out here, fear that made me sick and cold. I have the healthy man's dislike of death. I have no particular desire to be struck by a shell or a bullet, and up to now I have had only a nodding acquaintance with either. I am more or less afraid of them, but they do not strike terror into me. Once, when we were in the trenches, I was sentry on the parapet about one in the morning. The night was cold, there was a breeze crooning over the meadows between the lines, and the air was full of the sharp, penetrating odour of aromatic herbs. I felt tired and was half asleep as I kept a lazy look-out on the front where the dead are lying on the grass. Suddenly, away on the right, I heard a yell, a piercing, agonising scream, something uncanny and terrible. A devil from the pit below getting torn to pieces could not utter such a weird cry. It thrilled me through and through. I had never heard anything like it before, and hope I shall never hear such a cry again. I do not know what it was, no one knew, but some said that it might have been the yell of a Gurkha, his battle cry, when he slits off an opponent's head.

When I think of it, I find that my three thrills would be denied to a deaf man. The second occurred once when we were in reserve. The stench of the house in which the section was billeted was terrible. By day it was bad, but at two o'clock in the morning it was devilish. I awoke at that hour and went outside to get a breath of fresh air. The place was so eerie, the church in the rear with the spire battered down, the churchyard with the bones of the dead hurled broadcast by concussion shells, the ruined houses....As I stood there I heard a groan as if a child were in pain, then a gurgle as if some one was being strangled, and afterwards a number of short, weak, infantile cries that slowly died away into silence.

Perhaps the surroundings had a lot to do with it, for I felt strangely unnerved. Where did the cries come from ? It was impossible to say. It might have been a cat or a dog, all sounds become different in the dark. I could not wander round to seek the cause. Houses were battered down, rooms blocked up, cellars filled with rubble. There was nothing to do but to go back to bed. Maybe it was a child abandoned by a mother driven insane by fear. Terrible things happen in war.

The third fear was three cries, again in the dark, when a neighbouring battalion sent out a working party to dig a sap in front of our lines.

I could hear their picks and shovels busy in front, and suddenly somebody screamed "Oh! Oh! Oh!" the first loud and piercing, the others weaker and lower. But the exclamation told of intense agony. Afterwards I heard that a boy had been shot through the belly.

"I never like the bloomin' trenches," said Bill. "It almost makes me pray every time I go up."

"They're not really so bad," said Pryor, "some of them are quite cushy (nice)."

"Cushy!" exclaimed Bill, flicking the ash from his cigarette with the tip of his little finger. "Nark it, Pryor, nark it, blimey, they are cushy if one's not caught with a shell goin' in, if one's not bombed from the sky or mined from under the ground, if a sniper doesn't snipe 'arf yer 'ead off, or gas doesn't send you to 'eaven, or flies send you to the 'orspital with disease, or rifle grenades, pip-squeaks, and whizz-bangs don't blow your brains out when you lie in the bottom of the trench with yer nose to the ground like a rat in a trap. If it wasn't for these things, and a few more, the trench wouldn't be such a bad locality."

He put a finger and a thumb into my cigarette case, drew out a fag, and lit it off the stump of his old one. He blew a puff of smoke into the air, stuck his thumbs behind his cartridge pouches, and fixed a look of pity on Pryor.

"What are the few more things that you did not mention, Bill?" I asked.

"Few! Blimey, I should say millions. There's the stink of the dead men as well as the stink of the cheese, there's the dug-outs with the rain comin' in and the muck fallin' into your tea, the vermin, the bloke snorin' as won't let you to sleep, the fatigues that come when ye're goin' to 'ave a snooze, the rations late arrivin' and 'arf poisonin' you when they come, the sweepin' and brushin' of the trenches, work for a 'ousemaid and not a soldier, and the ——"

Bill paused, sweating at every pore.

"Strike me ginger, balmy, and stony," Bill concluded, "if it were not for these few things the life in the trenches would be one of the cushiest in the world."

CHAPTER IX

The Dug-out Banquet

You ask me if the trench is safe?
As safe as home, I say;
Dug-outs are safest things on land,
And 'buses running to the Strand
Are not as safe as they.

You ask me if the trench is deep?
Quite deep enough for me,
And men can walk where fools would creep,
And men can eat and write and sleep
And hale and happy be.

THE dug-out is the trench villa, the soldiers' home, and is considered to be proof against shrapnel bullets and rifle fire. Personally, I do not think much of our dug-outs, they are jerry-built things, loose in construction, and fashioned in haste. We have kept on improving them, remedying old defects, when we should have taken the whole thing to pieces and started afresh. The French excel us in fashioning dug-outs; they dig out, we build. They begin to burrow from the trench downwards, and the roof of their shelter is on a line with the floor of the trench; thus they have a cover over them seven or eight feet in thickness; a mass of earth which the heaviest shell can hardly pierce through. We have been told that the German trenches are even more secure, and are roofed with bricks, which cause a concussion shell to burst immediately it strikes, thus making the projectile lose most of its burrowing power. One of our heaviest shells struck an enemy's dug-out fashioned on this pattern, with the result that two of the residents were merely scratched. The place was packed at the time.

As I write I am sitting in a dug-out built in the open by the French. It is a log construction, built of pit-props from a neighbouring coal-mine. Short blocks of wood laid criss-cross form walls four feet in thickness; the roof is quite as thick, and the logs are much longer. Yesterday morning, while we were still asleep, a four-inch shell landed on the top, displaced several logs, but did us no harm. The same shell (pipsqueaks we call them) striking the roof of one of our trench dug-outs would blow us all to atoms.

The dug-out is not peculiar to the trench. For miles back from the firing-line the country is a world of dug-outs; they are everywhere, by the roadsides, the canals, and farmhouses, in the fields, the streets, and the gardens. Cellars serve for the same purpose. A fortnight ago my section was billeted in a house in a mining town, and the enemy began to shell the place about midnight. Bootless, half-naked, and half-asleep, we hurried into the cellar. The place was a regular Black Hole of Calcutta. It was very small, damp, and smelt of queer things, and there were six soldiers, the man of the house, his wife, and seven children, one a sucking babe two months old, cooped up in the place.

I did not like the place—in fact, I seldom like any dug-out, it reminds me of the grave, the covering earth, and worms, and always there is a feeling of suffocation. But I have enjoyed my stay in one or two. There was a delightful little one, made for a single soldier, in which I stayed. At night when off sentry, and when I did not feel like sleeping, I read. Over my head I cut a niche in the mud, placed my candle there, pulled down over the door my curtain, a real good curtain, taken from some neighbouring chateau, spent a few moments watching the play of light and shadows on the roof, and listening to the sound of guns outside, then lit a cigarette and read. Old Montaigne in a dug-out is a true friend and a fine companion. Across the ages we held conversation as we have often done. Time and again I have read his books; there was a time when for a whole year I read a chapter nightly: in a Glasgow doss-house, in a king's castle, in my Irish home, and now in Montaigne's own country, in a little earthy dug-out, I made the acquaintance of the man again. The dawn broke to the clatter of bayonets on the fire position when I put the book aside and buckled my equipment for the stand-to hour.

The French trench dug-outs are not leaky, ours generally are, and the slightest shower sometimes finds its way inside. I have often awakened during the night to find myself soaked through on a floor covered with slush. When the weather is hot we sleep outside. In some cases the dug-out is handsomely furnished with real beds, tables, chairs, mirrors, and candlesticks of burnished brass. Often there are stoves built into the clayey wall and used for cooking purposes. In "The Savoy" dug-out, which was furnished after this fashion, Section 3 once sat down to a memorable dinner which took a whole day long to prepare; and eatables and wine were procured at great risk to life. Incidentally, Bill, who went out of the trenches and walked four kilometres to procure a bottle of *vin rouge* was rewarded by seven days' second field punishment for his pains.

Mervin originated the idea in the early morning as he was dressing a finger which he had cut when opening a tin of bully beef. He held up the bleeding digit and gazed at it with serious eyes.

"All for this tin of muck!" he exclaimed. "Suppose we have a good square meal. I think we could get up one if we set to work."

Stoner's brown eyes sparkled eagerly.

"I know where there are potatoes and carrots and onions," he said. "Out in a field behind Dead Cow Villa; I'm off; coming Pat?"

"Certainly, what are the others doing, Bill?"

"We must have fizz," said my friend," and money was forthwith collected for wine. Bill hurried away, his bandolier round his shoulder and his rifle at the slope; and Mervin undertook to set the place in order and arrange the dug-out for the banquet. Goliath dragged his massive weight over the parados and busied himself pulling flowers. Kore cleaned the mess-tins, and Pryor, artistic even in matters of food, set about preparing a menu-card.

When we returned from a search which was very successful, Stoner divested himself of tunic and hat, rolled up his shirt sleeves, and got on with the cooking. I took his turn at sentry-go, and Z—, sleeping on the banquette, roused his stout body, became interested for a moment, and fell asleep again. Bill returned with a bottle of wine and seven eggs.

"Where did you get them?" I asked.

"'Twas the 'en as 'ad laid one," he replied. "And it began to brag so much about it that I couldn't stand it, so I took the egg, and it looked so lonely all by itself in my 'and that I took the others to keep it company."

At six o'clock we sat down to dine.

Our brightly burnished mess-tin lids were laid on the table, a neatly folded khaki handkerchief in front of each for serviette. Clean towels served for tablecloths, flowers—tiger-lilies, snapdragons, pinks, poppies, roses, and cornflowers rioted in colour over the rim of a looted vase. In solitary state a bottle of wine stood beside the flowers, and a box of cigars, the gift of a girl friend, with the lid open disclosed the dusky beauties within. The menu, Pryor's masterpiece, stood on a wire stand, the work of Mervin.

Goliath seated at the table, was smiles all over, in fact, he was one massive good humoured smile, geniality personified.

"Anything fresh from the seat of war?" he asked, as he waited for the soup.

"According to the latest reports," Pryor answered, "we've gained an inch in the Dardanelles and captured three trenches in Flanders. We were forced to evacuate two of these afterwards."

"We miscalculated the enemy's strength, of course," said Mervin.

"That's it," Pryor cut in. "But the trenches we lost were of no strategic importance."

"They never are," said Kore. "I suppose that's why we lose thousands to take 'em, and the enemy lose as many to regain them."

"Soup, gentlemen," Stoner interrupted, bringing a steaming tureen to the table. "Help yourselves."

"Mulligatawny?" said Pryor sipping the stuff which he had emptied into his mess-tin, "I don't like this."

Menu

Soupes

Lentil Rifle Oil
Mess Tin Wash Out

Hors-d'œuvres

Four-by-two.

Entrèe

Bœuf-à-la-Brazier

Légumes.

Pinched pommes-de-terres.
Petits-pois

Salade

Dessert

1 Frog (hopped away)
Cerises-à la Creme (Suisse)
Groseilles.

Fromage

God Save the King
Gott Strafe the Cooks
Music by 'Casey Court

No. 3
Section
L.I.R.

"Wot," muttered Bill, "wot's wrong with it?"

"As soup its above reproach, but the name," said Pryor. "It's beastly."

"Wot's wrong with it?"

"Everything," said the artistic youth, "and besides I was fed as a child on mulligatawny, fed on it until I grew up and revolted. To meet it again here in a dug-out. Oh! ye gods!"

"I'll take it," I said, for I had already finished mine.

"Will you?" exclaimed Pryor, employing his spoon with Gargantuan zeal. "It's not quite etiquette."

As he spoke a bullet whistled through the door and struck a tin of condensed milk which hung by a string from the rafter. The bullet went right through and the milk oozed out and fell on the table.

"Waiter," said Goliath in a sharp voice, fixing one eye on the cook, and another on the falling milk.

"Sir," answered Stoner, raising his head from his mess-tin.

"What beastly stuff is this trickling down? You shouldn't allow this you know."

"I'm sorry," said Stoner, "you'd better ɪick it up."

" 'Ad 'e," cried Bill. " Wot will we do for tea ? " The Cockney held a spare mess-tin under the milk and caught it as it fell. This was considered very unseemly behaviour for a gentleman, and we suggested that he should go and feed in the servants' kitchen.

A stew, made of beef, carrots, and potatoes came next, and this in turn was followed by an omelette. Then followed a small portion of beef to each man, we called this chicken in our glorious game of make-believe. Kore asserted that he had caught the chicken singing *The Watch on the Rhine* on the top of a neighbouring chateau and took it as lawful booty of war.

" Chicken, my big toe ! " muttered Bill, using his clasp-knife for a tooth-pick. " It's as tough as a rifle sling. Yer must have got hold of the bloomin' weathercock."

The confiture was Stoner's greatest feat. The sweet was made from biscuits ground to powder, boiled and then mixed with jam. Never was anything like it. We lingered over the dish loud in our praise of the energetic Stoner. " By God, I'll give you a job as head-cook in my establishment at your own salary," said Pryor. " Strike me ginger, pink, and crimson if ever I ate anything like it," exclaimed Bill. "We must 'ave a bit of this at every meal from now till the end of the war."

Coffee, wine, and cigars came in due course, then Section 3 clamoured for an address.

"Ool give it?" asked Bill.

"Pat," said Mervin.

"Come on Pat," chorused Section 3.

I never made a speech in my life, but I felt that this was the moment to do something. I got to my feet.

"Boys," I said, "it is a pleasure to rise and address you, although you haven't shaved for days, and your faces remind me every time I look at them of our rather sooty mess-tins."

(Bill: "Wot of yer own phiz.")

"Be quiet, Bill," I said, and continued. "Of course, none of you are to blame for the adhesive qualities of mud, it must stick somewhere, and doubtless it preferred your faces; but you should have shaved; the two hairs on Pryor's upper lip are becoming very prominent."

"Under a microscope," said Mervin.

"Hold your tongue," I shouted, and Mervin made a mock apology. "To-night's dinner was a grand success," I said, "all did their work admirably."

"All but you," muttered Bill, "yer spent 'arf the time writin' when yer should have been peelin' taters or pullin' onions."

"I resent the imputation of the gentleman at the rear," I said, "if I wasn't peeling potatoes and grinding biscuits I was engaged in chronicling the doings of Section 3. I can't make you fat and famous at the same time, much though I'd like to do both. You are an estimable body of men; Goliath, the big elephant—

(Goliath: "Just a baby elephant, Pat.")

"Mervin, who has travelled far and who loves bully stew; Pryor who dislikes girls with thick ankles, Kore who makes wash-out puns, Bill who has an insatiable desire for fresh eggs, and Stoner—I see a blush on his cheeks and a sparkle in his brown eyes already—I repeat the name Stoner with reverence. I look on the mess-tins which held the confiture and almost weep—because it's all eaten. There's only one thing to be done. Gentlemen, are your glasses charged?"

"There's nothin' now but water," said Bill.

"Water shame," remarked the punster.

“ Hold your tongues,” I said, “ fill them with water, fill them with anything. Ready? To the Section cook, Stoner, long life and ability to cook our sweets evermore.”

We drank. Just as we had finished, our company stretcher-bearers came by the door, a pre-occupied look on their faces and dark clots of blood on their trousers and tunics.

“ What has happened ? ” I asked.

“ The cooks have copped it,” one of the bearers answered. “ They were cooking grub in a shed at the rear near Dead Cow Villa, and a pip-squeak came plunk into the place. The head cook copped it in the legs, both were broken, and Erney, you know Erney ? ”

“ Yes ? ” we chorused.

“ Dead,” said the stretcher-bearer. “ Poor fellow he was struck unconscious. We carried him to the dressing station, and he came to at the door. ‘ Mother ! ’ he said, trying to sit up on the stretcher. That was his last word. He fell back and died.”

There was a long silence. The glory of the flowers seemed to have faded away and the lighted cigars went out on the table. Dead! Poor fellow. He was such a clean, hearty boy, very obliging and kind. How often had he given me hot water, contrary to regulations, to pour on my tea.

"To think of it," said Stoner. "It might have been any of us! We must put these flowers on his grave."

That night we took the little vase with its poppies, cornflowers, pinks, and roses, and placed them on the black, cold earth which covered Erney, the clean-limbed, good-hearted boy. May he rest in peace.

CHAPTER X

A Nocturnal Adventure

Our old battalion billets still,
  Parades as usual go on.
We buckle in with right good will,
  And daily our equipment don
As if we meant to fight, but no!
  The guns are booming through the air,
The trenches call us on, but oh!
  We don't go there, we don't go there!

I HAVE come to the conclusion that war is rather a dull game, not that blood-curdling, dashing, mad, sabre-clashing thing that is seen in pictures, and which makes one fearful for the soldier's safety. There is so much of the "everlastin' waitin' on an everlastin' road." The road to the war is a journey of many stages, and there is much of what appears to the unit as loitering by the wayside. We longed for action, for some adventure with which to relieve the period of "everlastin' waitin'."

Nine o'clock was striking in the room downstairs and the old man and woman who live in the house were pottering about, locking doors, and putting the place into order. Lying on the straw in the loft we could hear them moving chairs and washing dishes; they have seven sons in the army, two are wounded and one is a prisoner in Germany. They are very old and are unable to do much hard work; all day long they listen to the sound of the guns "out there." In the evening they wash the dishes, the man helping the woman, and at night lock the doors and say a prayer for their sons. Now and again they speak of their troubles and narrate stories of the war and the time when the Prussians passed by their door on the journey to Paris. "But they'll never pass here again," the old man says, smoking the pipe of tobacco which our boys have given him. "They'll get smashed out there." As he speaks he points with a long lean finger towards the firing line, and lifts his stick to his shoulder in imitation of a man firing a rifle.

Ten o'clock struck. We were deep in our straw and lights had been out for a long time. I could'nt sleep, and as I lay awake I could hear corpulent Z—— snoring in the corner. Outside a wind was whistling mournfully and sweeping through the joists of the roof where the red tiles had been shattered by shrapnel. There was something melancholy and superbly grand in the night; the heaven was splashed with stars, and the glow of rockets from the firing line lit up the whole scene, and at intervals blotted out the lights of the sky. Here in the loft all was so peaceful, so quiet; the pair downstairs had gone to bed, they were now perhaps asleep and dreaming of their loved ones. But I could not rest; I longed to get up again and go out into the night.

Suddenly a hand tugged at my blanket, a form rose from the floor by my side and a face peered into mine.

"It's me—Bill," a low voice whispered in my ear.

"Well?" I interrogated, raising myself on my elbow.

"Not sleepin'?" mumbled Bill, lighting a cigarette as he flopped down on my blanket, half crushing my toes as he did so. "I'm not sleeping neither," he continued. "Did you see the wild ducks to-day?"

"On the marshes? Yes."

"Could we pot one?"

"Rubbish. We might as well shoot at the stars."

"I never tried that game," said Bill, with

mock seriousness. "But I'm goin' to nab a duck. Strike me balmy if I ain't."

"It'll be the guard-room if we're caught."

"If *we* are caught. Then you're comin'? I thought you'd be game."

I slipped into my boots, tied on my puttees, slung a bandolier with ten rounds of ball cartridge over my shoulder, and groped for my rifle on the rack beneath the shrapnel-shivered joists. Bill and I crept downstairs and stole out into the open.

"Gawd! that puts the cawbwebs out of one's froat," whispered my mate as he gulped down mighty mouthfuls of cold night air. "This is great. I couldn't sleep."

"But we'll never hit a duck to-night," I whispered, my mind reverting to the white-breasted fowl which we had seen in an adjoining marsh that morning when coming back from the firing line. "Its madness to dream of hitting one with a bullet."

"Maybe yes and maybe no," said my mate, stumbling across the midden and floundering into the field on the other side.

We came to the edge of the marsh and halted for a moment. In front of us lay a dark pool, still as death and fringed with long grass and osier beds. A mournful breeze blew across the place, raising a plaintive croon, half of resignation and half of protest from the osiers and grasses as it passed. A little distance away the skeleton of a house stood up naked against the sky, the cold stars shining through its shattered rafters. " 'Twas shelled like 'ell, that 'ouse," whispered Bill, leaning on his rifle and fixing his eyes on the ruined homestead. " The old man at our billet was tellin' some of us about it. The first shell went plunk through the roof and two children and the mother were bowled over."

" Killed ? "

" I should say so," mumbled my mate ; then, " There's one comin' our way." Out over the line of trenches it sped towards us, whistling in its flight, and we could almost trace by its sound the line it followed in the air. It fell on the pool in front, bursting as it touched the water, and we were drenched with spray.

" 'Urt ? " asked Bill.

" Just wet a little."

" A little ! " he exclaimed, gazing at the spot where the shell exploded. " I'm soaked to the pelt. Damn it, 'twill frighten the ducks."

" Have you ever shot any living thing ? " I

asked my mate as I tried to wipe the water from my face with the sleeve of my coat.

"Me! Never in my nat'ral," Bill explained. "But when I saw them ducks this mornin' I thought I'd like to pot one o' em."

"Its impossible to see anything now," I told him. "And there's another shell!"

It yelled over our heads and burst near our billet on the soft mossy field which we had just crossed. Another followed, flew over the roof of the dwelling and shattered the wall of an outhouse to pieces. Somewhere near a dog barked loudly when the echo of the explosion died away, and a steed neighed in the horse-lines on the other side of the marsh. Then, drowning all other noises, an English gun spoke and a projectile wheeled through the air and towards the enemy. The monster of the thicket awake from a twelve hour sleep was speaking. Bill and I knew where he was hidden; the great gun that the enemy had been trying to locate for months and which he never discovered. He, the monster of the thicket, was working havoc in the foeman's trenches, and day after day great searching shells sped up past our billet warm from the German guns, but always they went far wide of their mark. Never could they discover the locality of the terrifying ninety-pounder, he who slept all day in his thicket home, awoke at midnight and worked until dawn.

" That's some shootin'," said my mate as the shells shrieked overhead. " Blimey, they'll shake the country to pieces—and scare the ducks."

Along a road made of bound sapling-bundles we took our way into the centre of the marsh. Here all was quiet and sombre ; the marsh-world seemed to be lamenting over some ancient wrong. At times a rat would sneak out of the grass, slink across our path and disappear in the water, again ; a lonely bird would rise into the air and cry piteously as it flew away, and ever, loud and insistent, threatening and terrible, the shells would fly over our heads, yelling out their menace of pain, of sorrow and death as they flew along.

We killed no birds, we saw none, although we stopped out till the colour of dawn splashed the sky with streaks of early light. As we went in by the door of our billet the monster of the thicket was still at work, although no answering shells sped up from the enemy's lines. Up in the loft Z—— was snoring loudly as he lay asleep on the straw, the blanket tight round his body, his jaw hanging loosely, and an unlighted pipe on the floor by his side. Placing our rifles on the rack, Bill and I took off our bandoliers and lay down on our blankets. Presently we were asleep.

That was how Bill and I shot wild duck in the marshes near the village of—Somewhere in France.

CHAPTER XI

The Man with the Rosary

There's a tramp o' feet in the mornin',
There's an oath from an N.C.O.,
As up the road to the trenches
The brown battalions go:
Guns and rifles and waggons,
Transports and horses and men,
Up with the flush of the dawnin',
And back with the night again.

SOMETIMES when our spell in the trenches comes to an end we go back for a rest in some village or town. Here the *estaminet* or *débitant* (French as far as I am aware for a beer shop), is open to the British soldier for three hours daily, from twelve to one and from six to eight o'clock. For some strange reason we often find ourselves busy on parade at these hours, and when not on parade we generally find ourselves without money. I have been here for four months; looking at my pay book I find that I've been paid 25 fr. (or in plain English, one pound) since I have come to France, a country where the weather grows hotter daily, where the water is seldom drinkable, and where wine and beer is so cheap. Once we were paid five francs at five o'clock in the afternoon after five penniless days of rest in a village, and ordered as we were paid, to pack up our all and get ready to set off at six o'clock for the trenches. From noon we had been playing cards, and some of the boys gambled all their pay in advance and lost it. Bill's five francs had to be distributed amongst several members of the platoon.

"It's only five francs, anyway," he said. "Wot matter whether I spend it on cards, wine, or women. I don't care for soldierin' as a profession?"

"What is your profession, Bill?" Pryor asked; we never really knew what Bill's civil occupation was, he seemed to know a little of many crafts, but was master of none.

"I've been everything," he replied, employing his little finger in the removal of cigarette ash. "My ole man apprenticed me to a marker of 'ot cross buns, but I 'ad a 'abit of makin' the long end of the cross on the short side, an' got chucked out. Then I learned 'ow to jump through tin plates in order to make them nutmeg graters, but left that job after sticking plump in the middle of a plate. I had to stop there for three days without food or drink. They were thinnin' me out, see! Then I was a draughts manager at a bank, and shut the ventilators; after that I was an electric mechanic; I switched the lights on and off at night and mornin'; now I'm a professional gambler, I lose all my tin."

"You're also a soldier," I said.

"Course, I am," Bill replied. "I can present hipes by numbers, and knock the guts out of sand-bags at five hundred yards."

We did not leave the village until eight o'clock. It was now very dark and had begun to rain, not real rain, but a thin drizzle which mixed up with the flashes of guns, the glow of star-shells and the long tremulous glimmer of flashlights. The blood-red blaze of haystacks afire near Givenchy, threw a sombre haze over our line of march. Even through the haze, star-shells showed brilliant in their many different colours, red, green, and electric white. The French send up a beautiful light which bursts into four different flames that burn standing high in mid-air for three minutes; another, a parachute star, holds the sky for four minutes, and almost blots its more remote sisters from the heavens. The English and the Germans are content to fling rockets across and observe one another's lines while these flare out their brief meteoric life. The firing-line was about five miles away; the starlights seemed to rise and fall just beyond an adjacent spinney, so deceptive are they.

Part of our journey ran along the bank of a canal; there had been some heavy fighting the night previous, and the wounded were still coming down by barges, only those who are badly hurt come this way, the less serious cases go by motor ambulance from dressing station to hospital—those who are damaged slightly in arm or head generally walk. Here we encountered a party of men marching in single file with rifles, skeleton equipment, picks and shovels. In the dark it was impossible to distinguish the regimental badge.

"Oo are yer?" asked Bill, who, like a good many more of us, was smoking a cigarette contrary to orders.

"The Camberwell Gurkhas," came the answer. "Oo are yer?"

"The Chelsea Cherubs," said Bill. "Up workin'!"

"Doin' a bit between the lines," answered one of the working party. "Got bombed out and were sent back."

"Lucky dogs, goin' back for a kip (sleep)."

"'Ad two killed and seven wounded."

"Blimey!"

"Good luck, boys," said the disappearing file as the darkness swallowed up the working party.

The pace was a sharp one. Half a mile back from the firing-line we turned off to the left and took our way by a road running parallel to the trenches. We had put on our waterproof capes, our khaki overcoats had been given up a week before.

The rain dripped down our clothes, our faces and our necks, each successive star-light showed the water trickling down our rifle butts and dripping to the roadway. Stoner slept as he marched, his hand in Kore's. We often move along in this way, it is quite easy, there is lullaby in the monotonous step, and the slumbrous crunching of nailed boots on gravel.

We turned off the road where it runs through the rubble and scattered bricks, all that remains of the village of Givenchy, and took our way across a wide field. The field was under water in the wet season, and a brick pathway had been built across it. Along this path we took our way. A strong breeze had risen and was swishing our waterproofs about our bodies; the darkness was intense, I had to strain my eyes to see the man in front, Stoner. In the darkness he was a nebulous dark bulk that sprang into bold relief when the starlights flared in front. When the flare died out we stumbled forward into pitch dark nothingness. The pathway was barely two feet across, a mere tight-rope in the wide waste, and on either side nothing stood out to give relief to the desolate scene; over us the clouds hung low, shapeless and gloomy, behind was the darkness, in front when the starlights made the darkness visible they only increased the sense of solitude.

We stumbled and fell, rose and fell again, our capes spreading out like wings and our rifles falling in the mud. The sight of a man or woman falling always makes me laugh. I laughed as I fell, as Stoner fell, as Mervin, Goliath, Bill, or Pryor fell. Sometimes we fell singly, again in pairs, often we fell together a heap of rifles, khaki, and waterproof capes. We rose grumbling, spitting mud and laughing. Stoner was very unfortunate, a particle of dirt got into his eye almost blinding him. Afterwards he crawled along, now and again getting to his feet, merely to fall back into his earthy position. A rifle fire opened on us from the front, and bullets whizzed past our ears, voices mingled with the ting of searching bullets.

"Anybody hurt ?"

"No, all right so far."

"Stoner's down."

"He's up again."

"Blimey, it's a balmy."

"Mervin's crawling on his hands and knees."

"Nark the doin's, ye're on my waterproof. Let go !"

"Goliath's down."

"Are you struck, Goliath ?"

"No, I wish to heaven I was," muttered the giant, bulking up in the flare of a searchlight, blood dripping from his face showed where he had been scratched as he stumbled.

We got safely into the trench and relieved the Highland Light Infantry. The place was very quiet, they assured us, it is always the same. It has become trench etiquette to tell the relieving battalion that it is taking over a cushy position. By this trench next morning we found six newly made graves, telling how six Highlanders had met their death, killed in action.

Next morning as I was looking through a periscope at the enemy's trenches, and wondering what was happening behind their sand-bag line, a man from the sanitary squad came along sprinkling the trench with creosote and chloride of lime.

"Seein' anything?" he asked.

"Not much," I answered, "the grass is so high in front that I can see nothing but the tips of the enemy's parapets. There's some work for you here," I said.

"Where?"

"Under your feet," I told him. "The floor is soft as putty and smells vilely. Perhaps there is a dead man there. Last night I slept by the spot and it turned me sick."

"Have you an entrenchin' tool?"

I handed him the implement, he dug into the ground and presently unearthed a particle of clothing, five minutes later a boot came to view, then a second; fifteen minutes assiduous labour revealed an evil-smelling bundle of clothing and decaying flesh. I still remained an onlooker, but changed my position on the banquette.

"He must have been dead a long time," said

the sanitary man, as he flung handfuls of lime on the body, " see his face."

He turned the thing on its back, its face up to the sky. The features were wonderfully well-preserved ; the man might have fallen the day before. The nose pinched and thin, turned up a little at the point, the lips were drawn tight round the gums, the teeth showed dog-like and vicious ; the eyes were open and raised towards the forehead, and the whole face was splashed with clotted blood. A wound could be seen on the left temple, the fatal bullet had gone through there.

" He was killed in the winter," said the sanitary man, pointing at the gloves on the dead soldier's hands. " These trenches were the ' Allemands ' then, and the boys charged 'em. I suppose this feller copped a packet and dropped into the mud and was tramped down."

" Who is he ? " I asked.

The man with the chloride of lime opened the tunic and shirt of the dead man and brought out an identity disc.

" Irish," he said, " Munster Fusiliers." " What's this ? " he asked, taking a string of beads with a little shiny crucifix on the end of it, from the dead man's neck.

"It's his rosary," I said, and my mind saw in a vivid picture a barefooted boy going over the hills of Corrymeela to morning Mass, with his beads in his hand. On either side rose the thatched cabins of the peasantry, the peat smoke curling from the chimneys, the little boreens running through the bushes, the brown Irish bogs, the heather in blossom, the turf stacks, the laughing colleens.... "

"Here's a letter," said the sanitary man, "it was posted last Christmas. It's from a girl, too."

He commenced reading :—

"My dear Patrick,—I got your letter yesterday, and whenever I was my lone the day I was always reading it. I wish the black war was over and you back again—we all at home wish that, and I suppose yourself wishes it as well ; I was up at your house last night ; there's not much fun in it now. I read the papers to your mother, and me and her was looking at a map. But we didn't know where you were so we could only make guesses. Your mother and me is making the Rounds of the Cross for you, and I am always thinking of you in my prayers. You'll be having the parcel I sent before you get this letter. I hope it's not broken or lost. The socks I sent were knitted by myself, three pairs of them, and I've put the holy water on them. Don't forget to put them on when your feet get wet, at home you never used to bother about anything like that ; just tear about the same in wet as dry. But you'll take care of yourself now, won't you : and not get killed ? It'll be a grand day when you come back, and God send the day to come soon ! Send a letter as often as you can, I myself will write you one every day, and I'll pray to the Holy Mother to take care of you."

We buried him behind the parados, and placed the rosary round the arms of the cross which was erected over him. On the following day one of our men went out to see the grave, and while stooping to place some flowers on it he got shot through the head. That evening he was buried beside the Munster Fusilier.

CHAPTER XII

The Shelling of the Keep

A brazier fire at twilight,
And glow-worm fires ashine,
A searchlight sweeping heaven,
Above the firing-line.
The rifle bullet whistles
The message that it brings
Of death and desolation
To common folk and kings.

WE went back from the trenches as reserves to the Keep. Broken down though the place was when we entered it there was something restful in the brown bricks, hidden in ivy, in the well-paved yard, and the glorious riot of flowers. Most of the original furniture remained—the beds, the chairs, and the pictures. All were delighted with the place, Mervin particularly. "I'll make my country residence here after the war," he said.

On the left was a church. Contrary to orders I spent an hour in the dusk of the first evening in the ruined pile. The place had been shelled for seven months, not a day had passed when it was not struck in some part. The sacristy was a jumble of prayer books, vestments, broken rosaries, crucifixes, and pictures. An ink pot and pen lay on a broken table beside a blotting pad. A lamp which once hung from the roof was beside them, smashed to atoms. In the church the altar railing was twisted into shapeless bars of iron, bricks littered the altar steps, the altar itself even, and bricks, tiles, and beams were piled high in the body of the church.

Outside in the graveyard the graves lay open and the bones of the dead were scattered broadcast over the green grass. Crosses were smashed or wrenched out of the ground and flung to earth; near the Keep was the soldiers' cemetery, the resting place of French, English, Indian, and German soldiers. Many of the French had bottles of holy water placed on their graves under the crosses. The English epitaphs were short and concise, always the same in manner: "Private 999 J. Smith, 26th London Battalion, killed in action 1st March, 1915." And under it stamped on a bronze plate was the information, "Erected by the Mobile Unit (B.R.C.S.) to preserve the record found on the spot." Often the dead man's regiment left a token of remembrance, a bunch of flowers, the dead man's cap or bayonet and rifle (these two latter only if they had been badly damaged when the man died). Many crosses had been taken from the churchyard and placed over these men. One of them read, "A notre dévote fille," and another, "To my beloved mother."

Several Indians, men of the Bengal Mountain Battery, were buried here. A woman it was stated, had disclosed their location to the enemy, and the billet in which they were staying was struck fair by a high explosive shell. Thirty-one were killed. They were now at rest—Anaytullah, Lakhasingh, and other strange men with queer names under the crosses fashioned from biscuit boxes. On the back of Anaytullah's cross was the wording in black: "Biscuits, 50 lbs."

Thus the environment of the Keep: the enemy's trenches were about eight hundred yards away. No fighting took place here, the men's rifles stood loaded, but no shot was fired; only when the front line was broken, if that ever took place, would the defenders of the Keep come into play and hold the enemy back as long as that were possible. Then when they could no longer hold out, when the foe pressed in on all sides, there was something still to do, something vitally important which would cost the enemy many lives, and, if a miracle did not happen, something which would wipe out the defenders for ever. This was the Keep.

The evening was very quiet; a few shells flew wide overhead, and now and again stray bullets pattered against the masonry. We cooked our food in the yard, and, sitting down amidst the flowers, we drank our tea and ate our bread and jam. The first flies were busy, they flew amidst the flower-beds and settled on our jam. Mervin told a story of a country where he had been in, and where the flies were legion and ate the eyes out of horses. The natives there wore corks hung by strings from their caps, and these kept the flies away.

"How?" asked Bill.

"The corks kept swinging backwards and forwards as the men walked," said Mervin. "Whenever a cork struck a fly it dashed the insect's brains out."

"Blimey!" cried Bill, then asked, "What was the most wonderful thing you ever seen, Mervin?"

"The most wonderful thing," repeated Mervin. "Oh, I'll tell you. It was the way they buried the dead out in Klondike. The snow lies there for six months and it's impossible to dig, so when a man died they sharpened his toes and drove him into the earth with a mallet."

"I saw a more wonderful thing than that, and it was when we lay in the barn at Richebourg," said Bill, who was referring to a comfortless billet and a cold night which were ours a month earlier. "I woke up about midnight 'arf asleep. I 'ad my boots off and I couldn't 'ardly feel them I was so cold. 'Blimey!' I said, 'on goes my understandin's, and I 'ad a devil of a job lacing my boots up. When I thought I 'ad them on I could 'ear someone stirrin' on the left. It was my cotmate. 'Wot's yer gime?' he says. 'Wot gime?' I asks. 'Yer foolin' about with my tootsies,' he says. Then after a minute 'e shouts, 'Damn it ye've put on my boots.' So I 'ad, put on his blessed boots and laced them mistaking 'is feet for my own."

"We never heard of this before," I said.

"No, cos 'twas ole Jersey as was lying aside me that night, next day 'e was almost done in with the bomb."

"It's jolly quiet here," said Goliath, sitting back in an armchair and lighting a cigarette. "This will be a jolly holiday."

"I heard an artillery man I met outside, say that this place was hot," Stoner remarked. "The Irish Guards were here, and they said they preferred the trenches to the Keep."

"It will be a poor country house," said Mervin, "if it's going to be as bad as you say."

On the following evening I was standing guard in a niche in the building. Darkness was falling and the shadows sat at the base of the walls east of the courtyard. My niche looked out on the road, along which the wounded are carried from the trenches by night and sometimes by day. The way is by no means safe. As I stood there four men came down the road carrying a limp form on a stretcher. A waterproof ground-sheet lay over the wounded soldier, his head was uncovered, and it wobbled from side to side, a streak of blood ran down his face and formed into clots on the ear and chin. There was something uncannily helpless in the soldier, his shaking head, his boots caked brown with mud, the heels close together, the toes pointing upwards and outwards and swaying a little. Every quiver of the body betokened abject helplessness. The limp, swaying figure, clinging weakly to life, was a pathetic sight.

The bearers walked slowly, carefully, stepping

over every shell-hole and stone on the road. The sweat rolled down their faces and arms, their coats were off and their shirt sleeves rolled up almost to the shoulders. Down the road towards the village they pursued their sober way, and my eyes followed them. Suddenly they came to a pause, lowered the stretcher to the ground, and two of them bent over the prostrate form. I could see them feel the soldier's pulse, open his tunic, and listen for the beating of the man's heart, when they raised the stretcher again there was something cruelly careless in the action, they brought it up with a jolt and set off hurriedly, stumbling over shell-hole and boulder. There was no doubt the man was dead now; it was unwise to delay on the road, and the soldiers' cemetery was in the village.

In the evening we stood to arms in the Keep; all our men were now out in the open, and the officers were inspecting their rifles barely four yards away from me. At that moment I saw the moon, a crescent of pale smoke standing on end near the West. I felt in my pocket for money, but found I had none to turn.

"Have you a ha'penny?" I asked Mervin who was passing.

" What for ? "

" I want to turn it, you know the old custom."

" Oh, yes," answered Mervin, handing me a coin. " Long ago I used to turn my money, but I found the oftener I saw the moon the less I had to turn. However, I'll try it again for luck." So saying he turned a penny.

" Do any of you fellows know Marie Redoubt ? " an officer asked at that moment.

" I know the place," said Mervin, " it's just behind the Keep."

" Will you lead me to the place ? " said the officer.

" Right," said Mervin, and the two men went off.

They had just gone when a shell hit the building on my left barely three yards away from my head. The explosion almost deafened me, a pain shot through my ears and eyes, and a shower of fine lime and crumpled bricks whizzed by my face. My first thought was, " Why did I not put my hands over my eyes, I might have been struck blind." I had a clear view of the scene in front, my mates were rushing hither and thither in a shower of white flying lime ; I could see dark forms falling, clambering to their feet and falling again. One figure detached itself from the rest and came rushing towards me, by my side it tripped and fell, then rose again. I could now see it was Stoner. He put his hands up as if in protest, looked at me vacantly, and rushed round the corner of the building. I followed him and found him once more on the ground.

"Much hurt?" I asked, touching him on the shoulder.

"Yes," he muttered, rising slowly, "I got it there," he raised a finger to his face which was bleeding, "and there," he put his hand across his chest.

"Well, get into the dug-out," I said, and we hurried round the front of the building. A pile of fallen masonry lay there and half a dozen rifles, all the men were gone. We found them in the dug-out, a hole under the floor heavily beamed, and strong enough to withstand a fair sized shell. One or two were unconscious and all were bleeding more or less severely. I found I was the only person who was not struck. Goliath and Bill got little particles of grit in the face, and they looked black as chimney sweeps. Bill was cut across the hand, Kore's arm was bleeding.

"Where's Mervin?"

"He had just gone out," I said, "I was speaking to him, he went with Lieut. —— to Marie Redoubt."

I suddenly recollected that I should not have left my place outside, so I went into my niche again. Had Mervin got clear, I wondered? The courtyard was deserted, and it was rapidly growing darker, a drizzle had begun, and the wet ran down my rifle.

"Any word of Mervin?" I called to Stoner when he came out from the dug-out, and moved cautiously across the yard. There was a certain unsteadiness in his gait, but he was regaining his nerve; he had really been more surprised than hurt. He disappeared without answering my question, probably he had not heard me.

"Stretcher-bearers at the double."

The cry, that call of broken life which I have so often heard, faltered across the yard. From somewhere two men rushed out carrying a stretcher, and hurried off in the direction taken by Stoner. Who had been struck? Somebody had been wounded, maybe killed! Was it Mervin?

Stoner came round the corner, a sad look in his brown eyes.

"Mervin's copped it," he said, "in the head.

It must have been that shell that done it; a splinter, perhaps."

"Where is he?"

"He's gone away on the stretcher unconscious. The officer has been wounded as well in the leg, the neck, and the face."

"Badly?"

"No, he's able to speak."

Fifteen minutes later I saw Mervin again. He was lying on the stretcher and the bearers were just going off to the dressing station with it. He was breathing heavily, round his head was a white bandage, and his hands stretched out stiffly by his sides. He was borne into the trench and carried round the first traverse. I never saw him again; he died two days later without regaining consciousness.

On the following day two more men went: one got hit by a concussion shell that ripped his stomach open, another, who was on sentry-go got messed up in a bomb explosion that blew half of his side away. The charm of the courtyard, with the flower-beds and floral designs, died away; we were now pleased to keep indoors and allow the chairs outside to stand idle. All day long the enemy shelled us, most of the shells dropped outside and played havoc with the church; but the figure on the crucifix still remained, a symbol of something great and tragical, overlooking the area of destruction and death. Now and again a shell dropped on the flower-beds and scattered splinters and showers of earth against buildings and dug-outs. In the evening an orderly came to the Keep.

"I want two volunteers," he said.

"For what?" I asked him.

"I don't know," was the answer, "they've got to report immediately to Headquarters."

Stoner and I volunteered. The Headquarters, a large dug-out roofed with many sand-bags piled high over heavy wooden beams, was situated on the fringe of the communication trench five hundred yards away from the Keep. We took up our post in an adjacent dug-out and waited for orders. Over our roof the German shells whizzed incessantly and tore up the brick path. Suddenly we heard a crash, an ear-splitting explosion from the fire line.

"What's that?" asked Stoner. "Will it be a mine blown up?"

"Perhaps it is," I ventured. "I wish they'd stop the shelling, suppose one of these shells hit our dug-out."

"It would be all U.P. with us," said Stoner, trying to roll a cigarette and failing hopelessly. "Confound it," he said, "I'm all a bunch of nerves, I didn't sleep last night and very little the night before."

His eyebrows were drawn tight together and wrinkles were forming between his eyes; the old sparkle was almost entirely gone from them.

"Mervin," he said, "and the other two, the bloke with his side blown away. It's terrible."

"Try and have a sleep," I said, "nobody seems to need us yet."

He lay down on the empty sand-bags which littered the floor, and presently he was asleep. I tried to read Montaigne, but could not, the words seemed to be running up and down over the page; the firing seemed to have doubled in intensity, and the shells swept low almost touching the roof of the dug-out.

"Orderly!"

I stumbled out into the open, and a sharp penetrating rain, and made my way to the Headquarters. The adjutant was inside at the telephone speaking to the firing line.

"Hello! that the Irish?" he said. "Anything to report? The mine has done no damage? No, fifteen yards back, lucky! Only three casualties so far."

The adjutant turned to an orderly officer: "The mine exploded fifteen yards in front, three wounded. Are you the orderly?" he asked, turning to me.

"Yes, sir."

"Find out where the sergeant-major is and ask him if to-morrow's rations have come in yet."

"Where is the sergeant-major?" I asked.

"I'm not sure where he stays," said the adjutant. "Enquire at the Keep."

The trench was wet and slobbery, every hole was a pitfall to trap the unwary; boulders and sand-bags which had fallen in waited to trip the careless foot. I met a party of soldiers, a corporal at their head.

"This the way to the firing line?" he asked.

"You're coming from it!" I told him.

"That's done it!" he muttered. "We've gone astray, there's some fun up there!"

"A mine blown up?" I asked.

"'Twas a blow up," was the answer. "It almost deafened us, someone must have copped it. What's the way back?"

"Go past Gunner Siding and Marie Redoubt, then touch left and you'll get through."

"God! it's some rain," he said. "Ta, ta."

"Ta, ta, old man."

I turned into the trench leading to the Keep. The rain was pelting with a merciless vigour, and loose earth was falling from the sides to the floor of the trench. A star-light flared up and threw a brilliant light on the entrance of the Keep as I came up. The place bristled with brilliant steel, half a dozen men stood there with fixed bayonets, the water dripping from their caps on to their equipment.

"Halt! who goes there!" Pryor yelled out, raising his bayonet to the "on guard" position.

"A friend," I replied. "What's wrong here?"

"Oh, it's Pat," Pryor answered. "Did you not hear it?" he continued, "the Germans have broken through and there'll be fun. The whole Keep is manned ready."

"Is the pantomime parapet manned?" I asked. I alluded to the flat roof of the stable in which our Section slept. It had been damaged by shell fire, and was holed in several places, a sand-bag parapet with loop-holes opened out on the enemy's front.

"Kore, Bill, Goliath, they're all up there," said Pryor, "and the place is getting shelled too, in the last five minutes twenty shells have missed the place, just missed it."

"Where does the sergeant-major stick?" I asked.

"Oh, I don't know, not here I think."

The courtyard was tense with excitement. Half a dozen new soldiers were called to take up posts on the parapet, and they were rushing to the crazy stairs which led to the roof. On their way they overturned a brazier and showers of fine sparks rioted into the air. By the flare it was possible to see the rain falling slanting to the ground in fine lines that glistened in the flickering light. Shells were bursting overhead, flashing out into spiteful red and white stars of flame, and hurling their bullets to the ground beneath. Shell splinters flew over the courtyard humming like bees and seeming to fall everywhere. What a miracle that anybody could escape them!

I met our platoon sergeant at the foot of the stairs.

"Where does the sergeant-major hold out?"

"Down at Givenchy somewhere," he told me. "The Germans have broken through," he said. "It looks as if we're in for a rough night."

"It will be interesting," I replied, "I haven't seen a German yet."

Over the parapet a round head, black amidst a line of bayonets appeared, and a voice called down, "Sergeant!"

"Right oh!" said the sergeant, and rushed upstairs. At that moment a shell struck a wall at the back somewhere, and pieces of brick whizzed into the courtyard and clattered down the stair. When the row subsided Kore was helped down, his face bleeding and an ugly gash showing above his left eye.

"Much hurt, old man?" I asked.

"Not a blighty, I'm afraid," he answered.

A "blighty" is a much desired wound; one that sends a soldier back to England. A man with a "blighty" is a much envied person. Kore was followed by another fellow struck in the leg, and drawing himself wearily along. He assured us that he wasn't hurt much, but now and again he groaned with pain.

"Get into the dug-outs," the sergeant told them. "In the morning you can go to the village, to-night it's too dangerous."

About midnight I went out on the brick pathway, the way we had come up a few nights earlier. I should have taken Stoner with me, but he slept and I did not like to waken him. The enemy's shells were flying overhead, one following fast on another, all bursting in the brick path and the village. I could see the bright hard light of shrapnel shells exploding in the air, and the signal-red flash of concussion shells bursting ahead. Splinters flew back buzzing like angry bees about my ears. I would have given a lot to be back with Stoner in the dug-out ; it was a good strong structure, shrapnel and bullet proof, only a concussion shell falling on top would work him any harm.

The rain still fell and the moon—there was a bit of it somewhere—never showed itself through the close-packed clouds. For a while I struggled bravely to keep to the tight-rope path, but it was useless, I fell over first one side, then the other. Eventually I kept clear of it, and walked in the slush of the field. Half way along a newly dug trench, some three feet in depth, ran across my road ; an attack was feared at dawn, and a first line of reserves were in occupation. I stumbled upon the men. They were sitting well down, their heads lower than the parapet, and all seemed to be smoking if I could form judgment by the line of little glow-worm fires, the lighted cigarette ends that extended out on either hand. Somebody was humming a music-hall song, while two or three of his mates helped him with the chorus.

"Halt! who goes there?"

The challenge was almost a whisper, and a bayonet slid out from the trench and paused irresolutely near my stomach.

"A London Irish orderly going down to the village," I answered.

A voice other than that which challenged me spoke: "Why are you alone, there should be two."

"I wasn't aware of that."

"Pass on," said the second voice, "and be careful, it's not altogether healthy about here."

Somewhere in the proximity of the village I lost the brick path and could not find it again. For a full hour I wandered over the sodden fields under shell fire, discovering the village, a bulk of shadows thinning into a jagged line of chimneys against the black sky when the shells exploded, and losing it again when the darkness settled down around me. Eventually I stumbled across the road and breathed freely for a second.

But the enemy's fire would not allow me a very long breathing space, it seemed bent on battering the village to pieces. In front of me ran a broken-down wall, behind it were a number of houses and not a light showing. The road was deserted.

A shell exploded in mid-air straight above, and bullets sang down and shot into the ground round me. Following it came the casing splinters humming like bees, then a second explosion, the whizzing bullets and the bees, another explosion....

"Come along and get out of it," I whispered to myself, and looked along the road; a little distance off I fancied I saw a block of buildings.

"Run!"

I ran, "stampeded!" is a better word, and presently found myself opposite an open door. I flung myself in, tripped, and went prostrate to the floor.

Boom! I almost chuckled, thinking myself secure from the shells that burst overhead. It was only when the bees bounced on the floor that I looked up to discover that the house was roofless.

I made certain that the next building had a roof before I entered. It also had a door, this I shoved open and found myself amongst a number of horses and warm penetrating odour of dung.

"Now, 3008, you may smoke," I said, addressing myself, and drew out my cigarette case. My matches were quite dry; I lit one and was just putting it to my cigarette when one of the horses began prancing at the other end of the building. I just had a view of the animal coming towards me when the match went out and left me in the total darkness. I did not like the look of the horse, and I wished that it had been better bound when its master left it. It was coming nearer and now pawing the floor with its hoof. I edged closer to the door; if it were not for the shells I would go outside. Why was that horse allowed to remain loose in the stable? I tried to light another match, but it snapped in my fingers. The horse was very near me now; I could feel its presence, it made no noise, it seemed to be shod with velvet. The moment was tense, I shouted: "Whoa there, whoa!"

It shot out its hind legs and a pair of hoofs clattered on the wall beside me.

"Whoa, there! whoa there! confound you!" I growled, and was outside in a twinkling and into the arms of a transport sergeant.

"What the devil—'oo are yer ?" he blurted out.

"Did you think I was a shell ?" I couldn't help asking. "I'm sorry," I continued, "I came in here out of that beastly shelling."

"Very wise," said the sergeant, getting quickly into the stable.

"One of your horses is loose," I said. "Do you know where the London Irish is put up here ?"

"Down the road on the right," he told me, "you come to a large gate there on the left and you cross a garden. It's a big buildin'."

"Thank you. Good night."

"Good night, sonny."

I went in by the wrong gate; there were so many on the left, and found myself in a dark spinney where the rain was dripping heavily from the branches of the trees. I was just on the point of turning back to the road when one of our batteries concealed in the place opened fire, and a perfect hell of flame burst out around me. I flopped to earth with graceless precipitancy, and wallowed in mud. "It's all up 3008, you've done it now," I muttered, and wondered vaguely whether I was partly or wholly dead. The sharp smell of cordite filled the air and caused a tickling sensation in my throat that almost choked me. When I scrambled to my feet again and found myself uninjured, a strange dexterity had entered my legs; I was outside the gate in the space of a second.

Ten minutes later I found the sergeant-major, who rose from a blanket on the ground-floor of a pretentious villa with a shell splintered door, rubbing the sleep from his eyes. The rations had not arrived; they would probably be in by dawn. Had I seen the mine explode? I belonged to the company holding the Keep, did I not? The rumour about the Germans breaking through was a cock-and-bull story. Had I any cigarettes? Turkish! Not bad for a change. Good luck, sonny! Take care of yourself going back.

I came in line with the rear trench on my way back.

"Who's there?" came a voice from the line of little cigarette lights.

"A London Irish orderly—going home!" I answered, and a laugh rewarded my ironical humour.

"Jolly luck to be able to return home," I said to myself when I got past. "3008, you weren't very brave to-night. By Jove, you did hop into that roofless house and scamper out of that spinney! In fact, you did not shine as a soldier at all. You've not been particularly afraid of shell fire before, but to-night! Was it because you were alone you felt so very frightened? You've found out you've been posing a little before. Alone you're really a coward."

I felt a strange delight in saying these things; the firing had ceased; it was still raining heavily.

"Remember the bridge at Suicide Corner," I said, alluding to a recent incident when I had walked upright across a bridge, exposed to the enemy's rifle fire. My mates hurried across almost bent double whilst I sauntered slowly over in front of them. "You had somebody to look at you then; 'twas vanity that did it, but to-night! You were afraid, terribly funky. If there had been somebody to look on, you'd have been defiantly careless. It's rather nerve-racking to be shelled when you're out alone at midnight and nobody looking at you!"

Dawn was breaking when I found myself at the Keep. The place in some manner fascinated me and I wanted to know what had happened there. I found that a few shells were still coming that way and most of the party were in their dug-outs. I peered down the one which was under my old sleeping place ; at present all stayed in their dug-outs when off duty. They were ordered to do so, but none of the party were sleeping now, the night had been too exciting.

" 'Oo's there ? " Bill called up out of the darkness, and when I spoke he muttered :

" Oh, it's ole Pat ! Where were yer ? "

" I've been out for a walk," I replied.

" When that shellin' was goin' on ? "

" Yes."

" You're a cool beggar, you are ! " said Bill. " I was warm here I tell yer ! "

" Have the Germans come this way ? " I asked.

" Germans ! " ejaculated Bill. " They come 'ere and me with ten rounds in the magazine and one in the breech ! They knows better ! "

Stoner was awake when I returned to the dug-out by Headquarters.

" Up already ? " I asked.

" Up ! I've been up almost since you went away," he answered. " My ! the shells didn't half fly over here. And I thought you'd never get back."

"That's due to lack of imagination," I told him. "What's for breakfast?"

CHAPTER XIII

A Night of Horror

'Tis only a dream in the trenches,
Told when the shadows creep,
Over the friendly sandbags
When men in the dug-outs sleep.
This is the tale of the trenches
Told when the shadows fall,
By little Hughie of Dooran,
Over from Donegal.

ON the noon following the journey to the village I was sent back to the Keep; that night our company went into the firing trench again. We were all pleased to get there; any place was preferable to the block of buildings in which we had lost so many of our boys. On the night after our departure, two Engineers who were working at the Keep could not find sleeping place in the dug-outs, and they slept on the spot where I made my bed the first night I was there. In the early morning a shell struck the wall behind them and the poor fellows were blown to atoms.

For three days we stayed in the trenches, narrow, suffocating and damp places, where parados and parapet almost touched and where it was well-nigh impossible for two men to pass. Food was not plentiful here, all the time we lived on bully beef and biscuits; our tea ran short and on the second day we had to drink water at our meals. From our banquette it was almost impossible to see the enemy's position; the growing grass well nigh hid their lines; occasionally by standing tiptoed on the banquette we could catch a glimpse of white sandbags looking for all the world like linen spread out to dry on the grass. But the Germans did not forget that we were near, pip-squeaks, rifle grenades, bombs and bullets came our way with aggravating persistence. It was believed that the Prussians, spiteful beggars that they are, occupied the position opposite. In these trenches the dug-outs were few and far between; we slept very little.

On the second night I was standing sentry on the banquette. My watch extended from twelve to one, the hour when the air is raw and the smell of the battle line is penetrating. The night was pitch black; in ponds and stagnant streams in the vicinity frogs were chuckling. Their hoarse clucking could be heard all round; when the star-shells flew up I could catch vague glimpses of the enemy's sandbags and the line of tall shrapnel-swept trees which ran in front of his trenches. The sleep was heavy in my eyes; time and again I dozed off for a second only to wake up as a shell burst in front or swept by my head. It seemed impossible to remain awake, often I jumped down to the floor of the trench, raced along for a few yards, then back to the banquette and up to the post beside my bayonet.

One moment of quiet and I dropped into a light sleep. I punched my hands against the sandbags until they bled; the whizz of the shells passed like ghosts above me; slumber sought me and strove to hold me captive. I had dreams; a village standing on a hill behind the opposite trench became peopled; it was summer and the work of haying and harvesting went on. The men went out to the meadows with long-handled scythes and mowed the grass down in great swathes. I walked along a lane leading to the field and stopped at the stile and looked in. A tall youth who seemed strangely familiar was mowing. The sweat streamed down his face and bare chest. His shirt was folded neatly back and his sleeves were thrust up almost to the shoulders.

The work did not come easy to him; he always followed the first sweep of the scythe with a second which cropped the grass very close to the ground. For an expert mower the second stroke is unnecessary; the youngster had not learned to put a keen edge on the blade. I wanted to explain to him the best way to use the sharping stone, but I felt powerless to move: I could only remain at the stile looking on. Sometimes he raised his head and looked in my direction, but took no notice of me. Who was he? Where had I seen him before? I called out to him but he took no notice. I tried to change my position, succeeded and crossed the stile. When I came close to him, he spoke.

"You were long in coming," he said, and I saw it was my brother, a youngster of eighteen.

"I went to the well for a jug of water," I said, "But it's dry now and the three trout are dead at the bottom."

"'Twas because we didn't put a cross of green rushes over it last Candlemas Eve," he remarked. "You should have made one then, but you didn't. Can you put an edge on the scythe?" he asked.

"I used to be able before—before the—" I stopped feeling that I had forgotten some event.

"I don't know why, but I feel strange," I said, "When did you come to this village?"

"Village?"

"That one up there." I looked in the direction where the village stood a moment before, but every red-brick house with its roof of terracotta tiles had vanished. I was gazing along my own glen in Donegal with its quiet fields, its sunny braes, steep hills and white limewashed cottages, snug under their neat layers of straw.

The white road ran, almost parallel with the sparkling river, through a wealth of emerald green bottom lands. How came I to be here? I turned to my brother to ask him something, but I could not speak.

A funeral came along the road; four men carried a black coffin shoulder high; they seemed to be in great difficulties with their burden. They stumbled and almost fell at every step. A man carrying his coat and hat in one hand walked in front, and he seemed to be exhorting those who followed to quicken their pace. I sympathised with the man in front. Why did the men under the coffin walk so slowly? It was a ridiculous way to carry a coffin, on the shoulders. Why did they not use a stretcher? It would be the proper thing to do. I turned to my brother.

"They should have stretchers, I told him."

"Stretchers?"

"And stretcher-bearers."

"Stretcher-bearers at the double!" he snapped and vanished. I flashed back into reality again; the sentinel on the left was leaning towards me; I could see his face, white under the Balaclava helmet. There was impatience in his voice when he spoke.

"Do you hear the message?" he called.

"Right!" I answered and leant towards the man on my right. I could see his dark, round head, dimly outlined above the parapet.

"Stretcher bearers at the double!" I called. "Pass it along."

From mouth to mouth it went along the living wire; that ominous call which tells of broken life and the tragedy of war. Nothing is so poignant in the watches of the night as the call for stretcher-bearers; there is a thrill in the message swept from sentinel to sentinel along the line of sandbags, telling as it does, of some poor soul stricken down writhing in agony on the floor of the trenches.

For a moment I remained awake; then

phantoms rioted before my eyes; the trees out by the German lines became ghouls. They held their heads together in consultation and I knew they were plotting some evil towards me. What were they going to do? They moved, long, gaunt, crooked figures dressed in black, and approached me. I felt frightened but my fright was mixed with curiosity. Would they speak? What would they say? I knew I had wronged them in some way or another; when and how I did not remember. They came near. I could see they wore black masks over their faces and their figures grew in size almost reaching the stars. And as they grew, their width diminished; they became mere strands reaching form earth to heaven. I rubbed my eyes, to find myself gazing at the long, fine grasses that grew up from the reverse slope of the parapet.

I leant back from the banquette across the narrow trench and rested my head on the parados. I could just rest for a moment, one moment then get up again. The ghouls took shape far out in front now, and careered along the top of the German trench, great gaunt shadows that raced as if pursued by a violent wind. Why did they run so quickly? Were they afraid of something ? They ran in such a ridiculous way that I could not help laughing. They were making way, that was it. They had to make way. Why ?

" Make way ! "

Two stretcher-bearers stood on my right ; in front of them a sergeant.

" Make way, you're asleep," he said.

" I'm not," I replied, coming to an erect position.

" Well, you shouldn't remain like that, if you don't want to get your head blown off."

My next sentry hour began at nine in the morning ; I was standing on the banquette when I heard Bill speaking. He was just returning with a jar of water drawn from a pump at the rear, and he stopped for a moment in front of Spud Higgles, one of No. 4's boys.

" Mornin' ! How's yer hoppin' it ? " said Spud.

" Top over toe ! " answered Bill. " 'Ow's you ? "

" Up to the pink. Any news ? "

" Yer 'aven't 'eard it ? "

" What ? "

" The Brigadier 's copped it this mornin'."

" Oo ? "

" Our Brigadier."

" Git ! "

" 'S truth ! "

" Strike me pink ! " said Spud. " 'Ow ? "

" A stray bullet."

" Stone me ginger ! but one would say he'd a safe job."

" The bullet 'ad 'is number ! "

" So, he's gone west ! "

" He's gone west ! "

Bill's information was quite true. Our Brigadier while making a tour of inspection of the trenches, turned to the orderly officer and said : " I believe I am hit, here." He put his hand on his left knee.

His trousers were cut away but no wound was visible. An examination was made on his body and a little clot of blood was found over the groin on the right. A bullet had entered there and remained in the body. Twenty minutes later the Brigadier was dead.

Rations were short for breakfast, dinner did not arrive, we had no tea but all the men were quite cheerful for it was rumoured that we were going back to our billets at four o'clock in the afternoon. About that hour we were relieved by another battalion, and we marched back through the communication trench, past Marie Redoubt, Gunner Siding, the Keep and into a trench that circled along the top of the Brick Path. This was not the way out ; why had we come here ? had the officer in front taken the wrong turning ? Our billet there was such a musty old barn with straw littered on the floor and such a quaint old farmhouse where they sold newly laid eggs, fresh butter, fried potatoes, and delightful salad ! We loved the place, the sleepy barges that glided along the canal where we loved to bathe, the children at play ; the orange girls who sold fruit from large wicker baskets and begged our tunic buttons and hat-badges for souvenirs. We wanted so much to go back that evening ! Why had they kept us waiting ?

" 'Eard that ? " Bill said to me. " Two London battalions are goin' to charge to-night. They're passing up the trench and we're in 'ere to let them get by."

" About turn !"

We stumbled back again into the communication trench and turned to the left, to go out we should have gone to the right. What was happening ? Were we going back again ? No dinner, no tea, no rations and sleepless nights.

....The barn at our billet with the cobwebs on the rafters....the salad and soup....We weren't going out that night.

We halted in a deep narrow trench between Gunner Siding and Marie Redoubt, two hundred yards back from the firing trench. Our officer read out orders.

"The —— Brigade is going to make an attack on the enemy's position at 6.30 this evening. Our battalion is to take part in the attack by supporting with rifle fire."

Two of our companies were in the firing line ; one was in support and we were reserves ; we had to remain in the trench packed up like herrings, and await further instructions. The enemy knew the communication trench ; they had got the range months before and at one time the trench was occupied by them.

We got into the trench at the time when the attack took place ; our artillery was now silent and rapid rifle fire went on in front ; a life and death struggle was in progress there. In our trench it was very quiet, we were packed tight as the queue at the gallery door of a cheap music-hall on a Saturday night.

" Blimey, a balmy this ! " said Bill making frantic efforts to squash my toes in his desire to find a fair resting place for his feet. "I'm 'ungry. Call this the best fed army in the world. Dog and maggot all the bloomin' time. I need all the hemery paper given to clean my bayonet, to sharpen my teeth to eat the stuff. How are we goin' to sleep this night, Pat?"

"Standing."

"Like a blurry 'oss. But Stoner's all right," said Bill. Stoner was all right; somebody had dug a little burrow at the base of the traverse and he was lying there already asleep.

We stood in the trench till eight o'clock almost suffocated. It was impossible for the company to spread out, on the right we were touching the supports, on the left was a communication trench leading to the point of attack, and this was occupied by part of another battalion. We were hemmed in on all sides, a compressed company in full marching order with many extra rounds of ammunition and empty stomachs.

I was telling a story to the boys, one that Pryor and Goliath gave credence to, but which the others refused to believe. It was a tale of two trench-mortars, squat little things that loiter about the firing line and look for all the world like toads ready to hop off. I came on two of these the night before, crept on them unawares and found them speaking to one another.

"Nark it, Pat," muttered Bill lighting a cigarette. "Them talking. Git out!"

"Of course you don't understand," I said. "The trench-mortar has a soul, a mind and great discrimination," I told him.

"What's a bomb?" asked Bill.

"'Tis the soul finding expression. Last night they were speaking, as I have said. They had a wonderful plan in hand. They decided to steal away and drink a bottle of wine in Givenchy."

"Blimey!"

"They did not know the way out and at that moment up comes Wee Hughie Gallagher of Dooran; in his sea-green bonnet, his salmon-pink coat, and buff tint breeches and silver shoon and mounted one of the howitzers and off they went as fast as the wind to the wine-shop at Givenchy."

"'Oo's 'Ughie what dy'e call 'im of that place?"

"He used to be a goat-herd in Donegal once upon a time when cows were kine and eagles of the air built their nests in the beards of giants."

"Wot!"

" I often met him there, going out to the pastures, with a herd of goats before him and a herd of goats behind him and a salmon tied to the laces of his brogues for supper."

" I wish we 'ad somethin' for supper," said Bill.

" Hold your tongue. He has lived for many thousands of years, has Wee Hughie Gallagher of Dooran," I said, " but he hasn't reached the first year of his old age yet. Long ago when there were kings galore in Ireland, he went out to push his fortune about the season of Michaelmas and the harvest moon. He came to Tir-nan-Oge, the land of Perpetual Youth which is flowing with milk and honey."

" I wish this trench was ! "

" Bill ! "

" But you're balmy, chum," said the Cockney, " 'owitzers talkin' and then this feller. Ye're pullin' my leg."

" I'm afraid you're not intellectual enough to understand the psychology of a trench-howitzer or the temperament of Wee Hughie Gallagher of Dooran, Bill."

" 'Ad 'e a finance ? "*

" A what ? " I asked.

* Fiancée.

" Wot Goliath 'as, a girl at home."

" That's it, is it? Why do you think of such a thing?"

" I was trying to write a letter to-day to St. Albans," said Bill, and his voice became low and confidential. " But you're no mate," he added. " You were goin' to make some poetry and I haven't got it yet."

" What kind of poetry do you want me to make?" I asked.

" Yer know it yerself, somethin' nice like!"

" About the stars — "

" Star-shells if you like."

" Shall I begin now? We can write it out later."

" Righto!"

I plunged into impromptu verse.

I lie as still as a sandbag in my dug-out shrapnel proof,
My candle shines in the corner, and the shadows dance on the roof,
Far from the blood-stained trenches, and far from the scenes of war,
My thoughts go back to a maiden, my own little guiding star.

" That's 'ot stuff," said Bill.

I was on the point of starting a fresh verse when the low rumble of an approaching shell was heard; a messenger of death from a great German gun out at La Bassée. This gun was no stranger to us; he often played havoc with the Keep; it was he who blew in the wall a few nights before and killed the two Engineers. The missile he flung moved slowly and could not keep pace with its own sound. Five seconds before it arrived we could hear it coming, a slow, certain horror, sure of its mission and steady to its purpose. The big gun at La Bassée was shelling the communication trench, endeavouring to stop reinforcements from getting up to the firing lines and the red field between.

The shell burst about fifty yards away and threw a shower of dirt over us. There was a precipitate flop, a falling backwards and forwards and all became messed up in an intricate jumble of flesh, equipment, clothing and rifles in the bottom of the trench. A swarm of "bees" buzzed overhead, a few dropped into the trench and Pryor who gripped one with his hand swore under his breath. The splinter was almost red-hot.

The trench was voluble.

"I'm chokin'; get off me tummy."

"Your boot's on my face."

"Nobody struck?"

" Nobody."

" Gawd ! I hope they don't send many packets like that."

" Spread out a little to the left," came the order from an officer. " When you hear a shell coming lie flat."

We got to our feet, all except Stoner, who was still asleep in his lair, and changed our positions, our ears alert for the arrival of the next shell. The last bee had scarely ceased to buzz when we heard the second projectile coming.

" Another couple of steps. Hurry up. Down." Again we threw ourselves in a heap ; the shell burst and again we were covered with dust and muck.

" Move on a bit. Quicker ! The next will be here in a minute," was the cry and we stumbled along the narrow alley hurriedly as if our lives depended on the very quickness, When we came to a halt there was only a space of two feet between each man. The trench was just wide enough for the body of one, and all set about to sort themselves in the best possible manner A dozen shells now came our way in rapid succession. Some of the men went down on their knees and pressed their faces close to the ground like Moslems at prayer.

They looked for all the world like Moslems as the pictures show them, prostrate in prayer. The posture reminded me of stories told of ostriches, birds I have never seen, who bury their heads in the sand and consider themselves free from danger when the world is hidden from their eyes.

Safety in that style did not appeal to me; I sat on the bottom of the trench, head erect. If a splinter struck me it would wound me in the shoulders or the arms or knees. I bent low so that I might protect my stomach; I had seen men struck in that part of the body, the wounds were ghastly and led to torturing deaths. When a shell came near, I put the balls of my hands over my eyes, spread my palms outwards and covered my ears with the fingers. This was some precaution against blindness; and deadened the sound of explosion. Bill for a moment was unmoved, he stood upright in a niche in the wall and made jokes.

"If I kick the bucket," he said, "don't put a cross with ''E died for 'is King and Country' over me. A bully beef tin at my 'ead will do, and on it scrawled in chalk, ''E died doin' fatigues on an empty stomach.'"

"A cig.," he called, "'oo as a cig., a fag, a

dottle. If yer can't give me a fag, light one and let me look at it burnin.' Give Tommy a fag an' 'e doesn't care wot 'appens. That was in the papers. Blimey! it puts me in mind of a dummy teat. Give it to the pore man's pianner...."

"The what!"

"The squalling kid, and tell the brat to be quiet, just like they tell Tommy to 'old 'is tongue when they give 'im a cig. Oh, blimey!"

A shell burst and a dozen splinters whizzed past Bill's ears. He was down immediately another prostrate Moslem on the floor of the trench. In front of me Pryor sat, his head bent low, moving only when a shell came near, to raise his hands and cover his eyes. The high explosive shells boomed slowly in from every quarter now, and burst all round us. Would they fall into the trench? If they did! The La Bassée monster, the irresistible giant, so confident of its strength was only one amongst the many. We sank down, each in his own way, closer to the floor of the trench. We were preparing to be wounded in the easiest possible way. True we might get killed; lucky if we escaped! Would any of us see the dawn?....

One is never aware of the shrapnel shell

until it bursts. They had been passing over our heads for a long time, making a sound like the wind in telegraph wires, before one burst above us. There was a flash and I felt the heat of the explosion on my face. For a moment I was dazed, then I vaguely wondered where I had been wounded. My nerves were on edge and a coldness swept along my spine....No, I wasn't struck....

"All right, Pryor ?" I asked.

"Something has gone down my back, perhaps it's clay," he answered. "You're safe ?"

"I think so," I answered. "Bill."

"I've copped it," answered the Cockney. "Here in my back, it's burnin' 'orrid."

"A minute, matey," I said, tumbling into a kneeling position and bending over him. "Let me undo your equipment."

I pulled his pack-straps clear, loosened his shirt front and tunic, pulled the clothes down his back. Under the left shoulder I found a hot piece of shrapnel casing which had just pierced through his dress and rested on the skin. A black mark showed where it had burned in but little harm was done to Bill.

"You're all right, matey," I said. "Put on your robes again."

"Stretcher-bearers at the double," came the cry up the trench and I turned to Pryor. He was attending to one of our mates, a Section 3 boy who caught a bit in his arm just over the wrist. He was in pain, but the prospect of getting out of the trench buoyed him up into great spirits.

"It may be England with this," he said.

"Any others struck?" I asked Pryor who was busy with a first field dressing on the wounded arm.

"Don't know," he answered. "There are others, I think."

"Every man down this way is struck," came a voice; "one is out."

"Killed?"

"I think so."

"Who is he?"

"Spud Higgles," came the answer; then—"No, he's not killed, just got a nasty one across the head."

They crawled across us on the way to the dressing station, seven of them. None were seriously hurt, except perhaps Spud Higgles, who was a little groggy and vowed he'd never get well again until he had a decent drink of English beer, drawn from the tap.

The shelling never slackened; and all the missiles dropped perilously near; a circle of five hundred yards with the trench winding across it, enclosed the dumping ground of the German guns. At times the trench was filled with the acid stench of explosives mixed with fine lime flung from the fallen masonry with which the place was littered. This caused every man to cough, almost choking as the throat tried to rid itself of the foreign substance. One or two fainted and recovered only after douches of cold water on the face and chest.

The suspense wore us down; we breathed the suffocating fumes of one explosion and waited, our senses tensely strung for the coming of the next shell. The sang-froid which carried us through many a tight corner with credit utterly deserted us, we were washed-out things; with noses to the cold earth, like rats in a trap we waited for the next moment which might land us into eternity. The excitement of a bayonet charge, the mad tussle with death on the blood-stained field, which for some reason is called the field of honour was denied us; we had to wait and lie in the trench, which looked so like a grave, and sink slowly into the depths of depression.

Everything seemed so monstrously futile, so unfinished, so useless. Would the dawn see us alive or dead? What did it matter? All that we desired was that this were past, that something, no matter what, came and relieved us of our position. All my fine safeguards against terrible wounds were neglected. What did it matter where a shell hit me now, a weak useless thing at the bottom of a trench? Let it come, blow me to atoms, tear me to pieces, what did I care? I felt like one in a horrible nightmare; unable to help myself. I lay passive and waited.

I believe I dozed off at intervals. Visions came before my eyes, the sandbags on the parapet assumed fantastic shapes, became alive and jeered down at me. I saw Wee Hughie Gallagher of Dooran, the lively youth who is so real to all the children of Donegal, look down at me from the top of the trench. He carried a long, glistening bayonet in his hand and laughed at me. I thought him a fool for ever coming near the field of war. War! Ah, it amused him! He laughed at me. I was afraid; he was not; he was afraid of nothing. What would Bill think of him? I turned to the Cockney; but he knelt there, head to the earth, a motionless Moslem. Was he asleep? Probably he was; any way it did not matter.

The dawn came slowly, a gradual awaking from darkness into a cheerless day, cloudy grey and pregnant with rain that did not fall. Now and again we could hear bombs bursting out in front and still the artillery thundered at our communication trench.

Bill sat upright rubbing his chest.

"What's wrong?" I asked.

"What's wrong! Everythink," he answered. "There are platoons of intruders on my shirt, sappin' and diggin' trenches and Lord knows wot!"

"Verminous, Bill?"

"Cooty as 'ell," he said. "But wait till I go back to England. I'll go inter a beershop and get a pint, a gallon, a barrel —"

"A hogshead," I prompted.

"I've got one, my own napper's an 'og's 'ead," said Bill.

"When I get the beer I'll capture a coot, a big bull coot, an' make 'im drunk," he continued. "When 'e's in a fightin' mood I'll put him inside my shirt an' cut 'im amok. There'll be ructions; 'e'll charge the others with fixed bayonets an' rout 'em. Oh! blimey! will they ever stop this damned caper? Nark it. Fritz, nark yer doin's, ye fool."

Bill cowered down as the shell burst, then sat upright again.

"I'm gettin' more afraid of these things every hour, he said, "what is the war about?"

"I don't know," I answered.

"I'm sick of it," Bill muttered.

"Why did you join?"

"To save myself the trouble of telling people why I didn't," he answered with a laugh. "Flat on yer tummy, Rifleman Teake, there's another shell."

About noon the shelling ceased; we breathed freely again and discovered we were very hungry. No food had passed our lips since breakfast the day before. Stoner was afoot, alert and active, he had slept for eight hours in his cubby-hole, and the youngster was now covered with clay and very dirty.

"I'll go back to the cook's waggon at Givenchy and rake up some grub," he said, and off he went.

CHAPTER XIV

A Field of Battle

The men who stand to their rifles
See all the dead on the plain
Rise at the hour of midnight
To fight their battles again.

Each to his place in the combat,
All to the parts they played,
With bayonet brisk to its purpose,
With rifle and hand-grenade.

Shadow races with shadow,
Steel comes quick on steel,
Swords that are deadly silent,
And shadows that do not feel.

And shades recoil and recover,
And fade away as they fall
In the space between the trenches,
And the watchers see it all.

I LAY down in the trench and was just dropping off to sleep when a message came along the trench.

"Any volunteers to help to carry out wounded?" was the call.

Four of us volunteered and a guide conducted us along to the firing line. He was a soldier of the 23rd London, the regiment which had made the charge the night before; he limped a little, a dejected look was in his face and his whole appearance betokened great weariness.

"How did you get on last night?" I asked him.

"My God! my God!" he muttered, and seemed to be gasping for breath. "I suppose there are some of us left yet, but they'll be very few."

"Did you capture the trench?"

"They say we did," he answered, and it seemed as if he were speaking of an incident in which he had taken no part. "But what does it matter? There's few of us left."

We entered the main communication trench, one just like the others, narrow and curving round buttresses at every two or three yards. The floor was covered with blood, not an inch of it was free from the dark reddish tint.

"My God, my God," said the 23rd man, and he seemed to be repeating the phrase without knowing what he said. "The wounded have been going down all night, all morning and they're only beginning to come."

A youth of nineteen or twenty sat in a niche in the trench, naked to the waist save where a bandaged-arm rested in a long arm-sling.

"How goes it, matey?" I asked.

"Not at all bad, chummie," he replied bravely; then as a spasm of pain shot through him he muttered under his breath, "Oh! oh!"

A little distance along we met another; he was ambling painfully down the trench, supporting himself by resting his arms on the shoulders of a comrade.

"Not so quick, matey," I heard him say, "Go quiet like and mind the stones. When you hit one of them it's a bit thick you know. I'm sorry to trouble you."

"It's all right, old man," said the soldier in front. "I'll try and be as easy as I can."

We stood against the wall of the trench to let them go by. Opposite us they came to a dead stop. The wounded man was stripped to the waist, and a bandage, white at one time but now red with blood, was tied round his shoulder. His face was white and drawn except over his cheek bones. There the flesh, tightly drawn, glowed crimson as poppies.

"Have you any water to spare, chummy?" he asked.

"We've been told not to give water to wounded men," I said.

"I know that," he answered. "But just a drop to rinse out my mouth! I've lain out between the lines all night. Just to rinse my mouth, chummy!"

I drew the cork from my water bottle and held it to his lips, he took a mouthful, paused irresolutely for a moment and a greedy light shone in his eyes. Then he spat the water on the floor of the trench.

"Thank you, chummy, thank you," he said, and the sorrowful journey was resumed.

Where the road from the village is cut through by the trench we came on a stretcher lying on the floor. On it lay a man, or rather, part of a man, for both his arms had been blown off near the shoulders. A waterproof ground sheet, covered with mud lay across him, the two stumps stuck out towards the stretcher-poles. One was swathed in bandages, the other had come bare, and a white bone protruded over a red rag which I took to be a first field dressing. Two men who had been busy helping the wounded all morning and the night before carried the stretcher to here, through the tortuous cutting. One had now dropped out, utterly exhausted. He lay in the trench, covered with blood from head to foot and gasping. His mate smoked a cigarette leaning against the revêtement.

"Reliefs?" he asked, and we nodded assent.

"These are the devil's own trenches," he said. "The stretcher must be carried at arms length over the head all the way, even an empty stretcher cannot be carried through here."

"Can we go out on the road?" asked one of my mates; an Irishman belonging to another section.

"It'll be a damned sorry road for you if you go out. They're always shelling it."

"Who is he?" I asked pointing to the figure on the stretcher. He was unconscious; morphia, that gift of Heaven, had temporarily relieved him of his pain.

"He's an N.C.O., we found him lying out between the trenches," said the stretcher-bearer. "He never lost consciousness. When we tried to raise him, he got up to his feet and ran away, yelling. The pain must have been awful."

"Has the trench been captured?"

"Of course it has," said the stretcher-bearer, an ironical smile hovering around his eyes. "It has been a grand victory. Trench taken by Territorials, you'll see in the papers. And there'll be pictures too, of the gallant charge.

Heavens! they should see between the trenches where the men are blown to little pieces."

The cigarette which he held between his blood-stained fingers dropped to the ground; he did not seem to notice it fall.

We carried the wounded man out to the road and took our way down towards Givenchy. The route was very quiet; now and then a rifle bullet flew by; but apart from that there was absolute peace. We turned in on the Brick Pathway and had got half way down when a shell burst fifty yards behind us. There was a moment's pause, a shower of splinters flew round and above us, the stretcher sank towards the ground and almost touched. Then as if all of us had become suddenly ashamed of some intended action, we straightened our backs and walked on. We placed the stretcher on a table in the dressing-room and turned back. Two days later the armless man died in hospital.

The wounded were still coming out; we met another party comprised of our own men. The wounded soldier who lay on the stretcher had both legs broken and held in place with a rifle splint; he also had a bayonet tourniquet round the thick of his arm. The poor fellow was in great agony. The broken bones were touching one another at every move. Now and again he spoke and his question was always the same: " Are we near the dressing station yet ? "

That night I slept in the trench, slept heavily. I put my equipment under me, that kept the damp away from my bones. In the morning Stoner told an amusing story. During the night he wanted to see Bill, but did not know where the Cockney slept.

" Where's Bill ? " he said.

" Bill," I replied, speaking though asleep.

" Bill, yes," said Stoner.

" Bill," I muttered turning on my side, seeking a more comfortable position.

" Do you know where Bill is ? " shouted Stoner.

" Bill ! " I repeated again.

" Yes, Bill ! " he said, " Bill. B-i-double l, Bill. Where is here ? "

" He's here," I said getting to my feet and holding out my water bottle. " In here." And I pulled out the cork.

I was twitted about this all day. I remembered nothing of the incident of the water bottle although in some vague way I recollected Stoner asking me about Bill.

On the following day I had a chance of visiting the scene of the conflict. All the wounded were now carried away, only the dead remained, as yet unburied.

The men were busy in the trench which lay on the summit of a slope; the ground dipped in the front and rear. The field I came across was practically "dead ground" as far as rifle fire was concerned. Only one place, the wire front of the original German trench, was dangerous. This was "taped out" as our boys say, by some hidden sniper. Already the parados was lined with newly-made firing positions, that gave the sentry view of the German trench some forty or fifty yards in front. All there was very quiet now but our men were making every preparation for a counter attack. The Engineers had already placed some barbed wire down; they had been hard at it the night before; I could see the hastily driven piles, the loosely flung intricate lines of wire flung down anyhow. The whole work was part of what is known as "consolidation of our position."

Many long hours of labour had yet to be

expended on the trench before a soldier could sleep at ease in it. Now that the fighting had ceased for a moment the men had to bend their backs to interminable fatigues. The war, as far as I have seen it is waged for the most part with big guns and picks and shovels. The history of the war is a history of sandbags and shells.

CHAPTER XV

The Reaction

We are marching back from the battle,
Where we've all left mates behind,
And our officers are gloomy,
And the N.C.O.'s are kind,
When a jew's harp breaks the silence,
Purring out an old refrain;
And we thunder through the village
Roaring "Here we are again."

FOUR days later we were relieved by the Canadians. They came in about nine o'clock in the evening when we stood to-arms in the trenches in full marching order under a sky where colour wrestled with colour in a blazing flare of star-shells. We went out gladly and left behind the dug-out in which we cooked our food but never slept, the old crazy sandbag construction, weather-worn and shrapnel-scarred, that stooped forward like a crone on crutches on the wooden posts that supported it.

"How many casualties have we had?" I asked Stoner as we passed out of the village and halted for a moment on the verge of a wood, waiting until the men formed up at rear.

"I don't know," he answered gloomily. "See the crosses there," he said pointing to the soldiers' cemetery near the trees. "Seven of the boys have their graves in that spot; then the wounded and those who went dotty. Did you see X. of —— Company coming out?"

"No," I said.

"I saw him last night when I went out to the Quartermaster's stores for rations," Stoner told me. "They were carrying him out on their shoulders, and he sat there very quiet like looking at the moon.

"Over there in the corner all by themselves they are," Stoner went on, alluding to the graves towards which my eyes were directed. "You can see the crosses, white wood——"

"The same as other crosses?"

"Just the same," said my mate. "Printed in black. Number something or another, Rifleman So and So, London Irish Rifles, killed in action on a certain date. That's all."

"Why do you say 'Chummy' when talking to a wounded man, Stoner?" I asked. "Speaking to a healthy pal you just say 'mate.'"

"Is that so?"

"That's so. Why do you say it?"

"I don't know."

"I suppose because it's more motherly."

"That may be," said Stoner and laughed.

Quick march! The moon came out, ghostly, in a cloudy sky; a light, pale as water, slid over the shoulders of the men in front and rippled down the creases of their trousers. The bayonets wobbled wearily on the hips, those bayonets that once, burnished as we knew how to burnish them, were the glory and delight of many a long and strict general inspection at St. Albans; they were now coated with mud and thick with rust, a disgrace to the battalion!

When the last stray bullet ceased whistling over our heads, and we were well beyond the range of rifle fire, leave to smoke was granted. To most of us it meant permission to smoke openly. Cigarettes had been burned for quite a quarter of an hour before and we had raised them at intervals to our lips, concealing the glow of their lighted ends under our curved fingers. We drew the smoke in swiftly, treasured it lovingly in our mouths for some time then exhaled it slowly and grudgingly.

The sky cleared a little, but at times drifts of

grey cloud swept over the moon and blotted out the stars. On either side of the road lone poplars stood up like silent sentinels, immovable, and the soft warm breeze that touched us like a breath shook none of their branches. Here and there lime-washed cottages, roofed with patches of straw where the enemy's shells had dislodged the terra-cotta tiles, showed lights in the windows. The natives had gone away and soldiers were billeted in their places. Marching had made us hot; we perspired freely and the sweat ran down our arms and legs; it trickled down our temples and dropped from our eyebrows to our cheeks.

"Hang on to the step! Quick march! As you were! About turn!" some one shouted imitating our sergeant-major's voice. We had marched in comparative silence up to now, but the mimicked order was like a match applied to a powder magazine. We had had eighteen days in the trenches, we were worn down, very weary and very sick of it all; now we were out and would be out for some days; we were glad, madly glad. All began to make noises at the same time, to sing, to shout, to yell; in the night, on the road with its lines of poplars we became madly delirious, we broke free like a confused torrent from a broken dam. Everybody had something to say or sing, senseless chatter and sentimental songs ran riot; all uttered something for the mere pleasure of utterance; we were out of the trenches and free for the time being from danger.

Stoner marched on my right, hanging on his knees a little, singing a music hall song and smoking. A little flutter of ash fell from his cigarette, which seemed to be stuck to his lower lip as it rose and fell with the notes of the song. When he came to the chorus he looked round as if defying somebody, then raised his right hand over his head and gripping his rifle, held the weapon there until the last word of the chorus trembled on his lips; then he brought it down with the last word and looked round as if to see that everybody was admiring his action. Bill played his jew's harp, strummed countless sentimental, music-hall ditties on its sensitive tongue, his being was flooded with exuberant song, he was transported by his trumpery toy. Bill lived, his whole person surged with a vitality impossible to stem.

We came in line with a row of cottages, soldiers' billets for the most part, and the boys were not yet in bed. It was a place to sing something great, something in sympathy with our own mood. The song when it came was appropriate, it came from one voice, and hundreds took it up furiously as if they intended to tear it to pieces.

Here we are, here we are, here we are again.

The soldiers not in bed came out to look at us; it made us feel noble; but to me, with that feeling of nobility there came something pathetic, an influence of sorrow that caused my song to dissolve in a vague yearning that still had no separate existence of its own. It was as yet one with the night, with my mood and the whole spin of things. The song rolled on :—

Fit and well and feeling as right as rain,
Now we're all together; never mind the weather,
Since here we are again,
When there's trouble brewing; when there's something
doing,
Are we downhearted. No! let them all come!
Here we are, here we are, here we are again!

As the song died away I felt very lonely, a being isolated. True there was a barn with cobwebs on its rafters down the road, a snug farm where they made fresh butter and sold new laid eggs. But there was something in the night, in the ghostly moonshine, in the bushes out in the fields nodding together as if in consultation, in the tall poplars, in the straight road, in the sound of rifle firing to rear and in the song sung by the tired boys coming back from battle, that filled me with infinite pathos and a feeling of being alone in a shelterless world. "Here we are; here we are again." I thought of Mervin, and six others dead, of their white crosses, and I found myself weeping silently like a child....

CHAPTER XVI

PEACE AND WAR

You'll see from the La Bassée Road, on any summer day,
The children herding nanny goats, the women making hay.
You'll see the soldiers, khaki clad, in column and platoon,
Come swinging up La Bassée Road from billets in Bethune.
There's hay to save and corn to cut, but harder work by far
Awaits the soldier boys who reap the harvest fields of war.
You'll see them swinging up the road where women work at hay,
The long, straight road, La Bassee Road, on any summer day.

THE farmhouse stood in the centre of the village; the village rested on the banks of a sleepy canal on which the barges carried the wounded down from the slaughter line to the hospital at Bethune. The village was shelled daily. When shelling began a whistle was blown warning all soldiers to seek cover immediately in the dug-outs roofed with sandbags, which were constructed by the military authorities in nearly every garden in the place. When the housewifes heard the shells bursting they ran out and brought in their washing from the lines where it was hung out to dry; then they sat down and knitted stockings or sewed garments to send to their menfolk at the war. In the village they said: "When the shells come the men run in for their lives, and the women run out for their washing."

The village was not badly battered by shell fire. Our barn got touched once and a large splinter of a concussion shell which fell there was used as a weight for a wag-of-the-wall clock in the farmhouse. The village was crowded with troops, new men, who wore clean shirts, neat puttees and creased trousers. They had not been in the trenches yet, but were going up presently.

Bill and I were sitting in an *estaminet* when two of these youngsters came in and sat opposite.

"New 'ere?" asked Bill.

"Came to Boulogne six days ago and marched all the way here," said one of them, a red-haired youth with bushy eyebrows. "Long over?" he asked.

"Just about nine months," said Bill.

"You've been through it then."

"Through it," said Bill, lying splendidly, "I think we 'ave. At Mons we went in eight 'undred strong. We're the only two as is left."

"Gracious! And you never got a scratch?"

" Never a pin prick," said Bill, " And I saw the shells so thick comin' over us that you couldn't see the sky. They was like crows up above."

" They were ? "

" We were in the trenches then," Bill said. " The orficer comes up and sez : ' Things are getting despirate ! We've got to charge. 'Ool foller me ? " ' I'm with you ! ' I sez, and up I jumps on the parapet pulling a machine gun with me."

" A machine gun ! " said the red-haired man.

" A machine gun," Bill went on. " When one is risen 'e can do anything. I could 'ave lifted a 'ole battery on my shoulders because I was mad I 'ad a look to my front to get the position then I goes forward. ' Come back, cried the orficer as 'e fell——"

" Fell ! "

" 'E got a bullet through his bread basket and 'e flopped. But there was no 'oldin' o' me. 'Twas death or glory, neck 'an nothin', 'ell for leather at that moment. The London Irish blood was up ; one of the Chelsea Cherubs was out for red blood 'olesale and retail. I slung the machine gun on my shoulder, sharpened my bayonet with a piece of sand-paper, took the first line o' barbed wire entanglements at a jump and got caught on the second. It gored me like a bull. I got six days C.B. for 'avin' the rear of my trousers torn when we came out o' the trenches."

"Tell me something I can believe," said the red-haired youth.

"Am I not tellin' you something," asked Bill. "Nark it, matey, nark it. I tell Gospel-stories and you'll not believe me."

"But it's all tommy rot."

"Is it? The Germans did'nt think so when I charged plunk into the middle of 'em. Yer should 'ave been there to see it. They were all round me and two taubes over 'ead watching my movements. Swish! and my bayonet went through the man in front and stabbed the identity disc of another. When I drew the bayonet out the butt of my 'ipe * would 'it a man behind me in the tummy. Ugh! 'e would say and flop bringing a mate down with 'im may be. The dead was all round me and I built a parapet of their bodies, puttin' the legs criss-cross and makin' loop 'oles. Then they began to bomb me from the other side. 'Twas gettin' 'ot I tell you and I

* Rifle.

began to think of my 'ome ; the dug-out in the trench. What was I to do ? If I crossed the open they'd bring me down with a bullet. There was only one thing to be done. I had my boots on me for three 'ole weeks of 'ot weather, 'otter than this and beer not so near as it is now——"

"Have another drink, Bill ? " I asked.

"Glad yer took the 'int," said my mate. "Story tellin's a dry fatigue. Well as I was sayin' my socks 'ad been on for a 'ole month——"

"Three weeks," I corrected.

"Three weeks," Bill repeated and continued. "I took orf my boots. 'Respirators !' the Germans yelled the minute my socks were bare, and off they went leavin' me there with my 'ome-made trench. When I came back I got a dose of C.B. as I've told you before."

We went back to our billet. In the farmyard the pigs were busy on the midden, and they looked at us with curious expressive eyes that peered roguishly out from under their heavy hanging cabbage-leaves of ears. In one corner was the field-cooker. The cooks were busy making dixies of bully beef stew. Their clothes were dirty and greasy, so were their arms, bare from the shoulders almost, and taut with muscles. Through a path that wound amongst a medley of agricultural instruments, ploughs harrows and grubbers, the farmer's daughter came striding like a ploughman, two children hanging on to her apron strings. A stretcher leant against our water-cart, and dried clots of blood were on its shafts. The farmer's dog lay panting on the midden, his red tongue hanging out and saliva dropping on the dung, overhead the swallows were swooping and flying in under the eaves where now and again they nested for a moment before getting up to resume their exhilirating flight. A dirty bare-footed boy came in through the large entrance-gate leading a pair of sleepy cows with heavy udders which shook backwards and forwards as they walked. The horns of one cow were twisted, the end of one pointed up, the end of the other pointed down.

One of Section 4's boys was looking at the cow.

"The ole geeser's 'andlebars is twisted," said Bill, addressing nobody in particular and alluding to the cow.

"It's 'orns, yer fool!" said Section 4.

"Yer fool, yerself!" said Bill. "I'm not as big a fool as I look——"

" Git ! Your no more brains than a 'en."

" Nor 'ave you either," said Bill.

" I've twice as many brains, as you," said Section 4.

" So 'ave I," was the answer made by Bill ; then getting pugilistic he thundered out : " I'll give yer one on the moosh."

" Will yer ? " said Section 4.

" Straight I will. Give you one across your ugly phiz ! It looks as if it had been out all night and some one dancing on it."

Bill took off his cap and flung it on the ground as if it were the gauntlet of a knight of old. His hair, short and wiry, stood up on end. Section 4 looked at it.

" Your hair looks like furze in a fit," said Section 4.

" You're lookin' for one on the jor," said Bill closing and opening his fist. " And I'll give yer one."

" Will yer ? Two can play at that gyme ! "

Goliath massive and monumental came along at that moment. He looked at Bill.

" Looking for trouble, mate ? " he asked.

" Section 4's shouting the odds, as usual," Bill replied.

"Come along to the Canal and have a bath; it will cool your temper."

"Will it?" said Bill as he came along with us somewhat reluctantly towards the Canal banks.

"What does shouting the odds mean?" I asked him.

"Chewin' the rag," he answered.

"And that means——"

"Kicking up a row and lettin' every one round you know," said Bill. "That's what shoutin' the blurry odds means."

"What's the difference between shouting the odds and shouting the blurry odds?" I asked.

"It's like this, Pat," Bill began to explain, a blush rising on his cheeks. Bill often blushed. "Shoutin' the odds isn't strong enough, but shoutin' the blurry odds has ginger in it. It makes a bloke listen to you."

Stoner was sitting on the bank of La Bassée canal, his bare feet touching the water, his body deep in a cluster of wild iris. I sat down beside him and took off my boots.

I pulled a wild iris and explained to Stoner how in Donegal we made boats from the iris and placed them by the brookside at night.

When we went to bed the fairies crossed the streams on the boats which we made.

"Did they cross on the boats?" asked Stoner.

"Of course they did," I answered. "We never found a boat left in the morning."

"The stream washed them away," said Stoner.

"You civilised abomination," I said and proceeded to fashion a boat, when it was made I placed it on the stream and watched it circle round on an eddy near the bank.

"Here's something," said Stoner, getting hold of a little frog with his hand and placing it on the boat. For a moment the iris bark swayed unsteadily, the frog's little glistening eyes wobbled in its head then it dived in to the water, overturning the boat as it hopped off it.

An impudent-looking little boy with keen, inquisitive eyes, came along the canal side wheeling a very big barrow on which was heaped a number of large loaves. His coat a torn, ragged fringe, hung over the hips, he wore a Balaclava helmet (thousands of which have been flung away by our boys in the hot weather) and khaki puttees.

The boy came to a stop opposite, laid down his barrow and wiped the sweat from his brow with a dirty hand.

"Bonjour!" said the boy.

"Bonjour, petit garçon," Stoner replied, proud of his French which is limited to some twenty words.

The boy asked for a cigarette; a souvenir. We told him to proceed on his journey, we were weary of souvenir hunters. The barrow moved on, the wheel creaking rustily and the boy whistled a light-hearted tune. That his request had not been granted did not seem to trouble him.

Two barges, coupled and laden with coal rounded a corner of the canal. They were drawn by five persons, a woman with a very white sunbonnet in front. She was followed by a barefooted youth in khaki tunic, a hunch-backed man with heavy projecting jowl and a hare-lipped youth of seventeen or eighteen. Last on the tug rope was an oldish man with a long white beard parted in the middle and rusty coloured at the tips. A graceful slip of a girl, lithe as a marsh sapling, worked the tiller of the rear barge and she took no notice of the soldiers on the shore or in the water.

" Going to bathe, Stoner ? " I asked.

" When the barges go by," he answered and I twitted him on his modesty.

Goliath, six foot three of magnificent bone and muscle was in the canal. Swanking his trudgeon stroke he surged through the dirty water like an excited whale, puffing and blowing. Bill, losing in every stroke, tried to race him, but retired beaten and very happy. The cold water rectified his temper, he was now in a most amiable humour. Pryor was away down the canal on the barge, when he came to the bridge he would dive off and race some of Section 4 boys back to the spot where I was sitting. There is an eternal and friendly rivalry between Sections 3 and 4.

" Stoner, going in ? " I asked my comrade, who was standing stark on the bank.

" In a minute," he answered.

" Now," I said.

" Get in yourself ——"

" Presently," I replied, " but you go in now, unless you want to get shoved in."

He dived gracefully and came up near the other bank spluttering and shaking the water off his hair. Bill challenged him to a race and both struck off down the stream, as they swam passing jokes with their comrades on the bank. In the course of ten minutes they returned, perched proudly on the stern of a barge and making ready to dive. At that moment I undressed and went in.

My swim was a very short one ; shorter than usual, and I am not much of a swimmer. A searching shell sped over from the German lines hit the ground a few hundred yards to rear of the Canal and whirled a shower of dust into the water, which speedily delivered several hundred nude fighters to the clothes-littered bank. A second and third shell dropping nearer drove all modest thoughts from our minds for the moment (unclothed, a man feels helplessly defenceless), and we hurried into our warrens through throngs of women rushing out to take in their washing.

One of the shells hit the artillery horse lines on the left of the village and seven horses were killed.

CHAPTER XVII

Everyday Life at the Front

There's the butter, gad, and horse-fly,
The blow-fly and the blue,
The fine fly and the coarse fly,
But never flew a worse fly
Of all the flies that flew

Than the little sneaky black fly
That gobbles up our ham,
The beggar's not a slack fly,
He really is a crack fly,
And wolfs the soldiers jam.

So strafe that fly! Our motto
Is "strafe him when you can."
He'll die because he ought to,
He'll go because he's got to,
So at him every man!

WHAT time we have not been in the trenches we have spent marching out or marching back to them, or sleeping in billets at the rear and going out as working parties, always ready to move at two hours' notice by day and one hour's notice by night.

I got two days C.B. at La Beuvriere; because I did not come out on parade one morning. I really got out of bed very early, and went for a walk. Coming to a pond where a number of frogs were hopping from the bank into the water, I sat down and amused myself by watching them staring at me out of the pond; their big, intelligent eyes full of some wonderful secret. They interested and amused me, probably I interested and amused them, one never knows. Then I read a little and time flew by. On coming back I was told to report at the Company orderly room. Two days C.B.

I got into trouble at another time. I was on sentry go at a dingy place, a village where the people make their living by selling bad beer and weak wine to one another. Nearly every house in the place is an *estaminet.* I slept in the guardroom and as my cartridge pouches had an unholy knack of prodding a stomach which rebelled against digesting bully and biscuit, I unloosed my equipment buckles. The Visiting Rounds found me imperfectly dressed, my shoulder flaps wobbled, my haversack hung with a slant and the cartridge pouches leant out as if trying to spring on my feet. The next evening I was up before the C.O.

My hair was rather long, and as it was well-brushed it looked imposing. So I thought in the morning when I looked in the platoon mirror—the platoon mirror was an inch square glass with a jagged edge. My imposing hair caught the C.O.'s eye the moment I entered the orderly room. "Don't let me see you with hair like that again," he began and read out the charge. I forget the words which hinted that I was a wrong-doer in the eyes of the law military; the officers were there, every officer in the battalion, they all looked serious and resigned. It seemed as if their minds had been made up on something relating to me.

The orderly officer who apprehended me in the act told how he did it, speaking as if from a book but consulting neither notes nor papers.

"What have you to say?" asked the C.O. looking at me.

I had nothing particular to say, my thoughts were busy on an enigma that might not interest him, namely, why a young officer near him kept rubbing a meditative chin with a fugitive finger, and why that finger came down so swiftly when the C.O.'s eyes were turned towards the young man. I replied to the question by saying "Guilty."

"We know you are guilty," said the C.O. and gave me a little lecture. I had a reputation, the young men of the regiment looked up to me, an older man; and by setting a good example I could do a great deal of good, &c., &c. The lecture was very trying, but the rest of the proceedings were interesting. I was awarded three extra guards. I only did one of them.

We hung on the fringe of the Richebourge *mêlée,* but were not called into play.

"What was it like?" we asked the men men marching back from battle in the darkness and the rain. There was no answer, they were too weary even to speak.

"How did you get along in the fight?" I called to one who straggled along in the rear, his head sunk forward on his breast, his knees bending towards the ground.

"Tsch! Tsch!" he answered, his voice barely rising above a whisper as his boots paced out in a rhythm of despair to some village at the raer.

There in the same place a night later, we saw soldiers' equipments piled on top of one another and stretching for yards on either side of the road: packs, haversacks, belts, bayonets, rifles, and cartridge pouches. The equipments were taken in from the field of battle, the war-harness of men now wounded and dead was out of use for the moment, other soldiers would wear them presently and make great fight in them.

Once at Cuinchy, Section 3 went out for a wash in a dead stream that once flowed through our lines and those of the Germans. The water was dirty and it was a miracle that the frogs which frisked in it were so clean.

"It's too dirty to wash there," said Pryor.

"A change of dirt is 'olesome," said Bill, placing his soap on the bank and dipping his mess tin in the water. As he bent down the body of a dead soldier inflated by its own rottenness bubbled up to the surface. We gave up all idea of washing. Stoner who was on the opposite bank tried to jump across at that moment. Miscalculating the distance, he fell short and into the water. We dragged him out spluttering and I regret to say we laughed, almost heartily. That night when we stood to arms in the trenches, waiting for an attack that did not come off, Stoner stood to with his rifle, an overcoat, a pair of boots and a pair of socks as his sole uniform.

How many nights have we marched under the light of moon and stars, sleepy and dog-weary, in song or in silence, as the mood prompted us or the orders compelled us, up to the trenches and back again! We have slept in the same old barns with cobwebs in the roof and straw deep on the floor. We have sung songs, old songs that float on the ocean of time like corks and find a cradle on every wave; new songs that make a momentary ripple on the surface and die as their circle extends outwards, songs of love and lust, of murder and great adventure. We have gambled, won one another's money and lost to one another again, we have had our disputes, but were firm in support of any member of our party who was flouted by any one who was not one of WE. "Section 3, right or wrong" was and is our motto. And the section dwindles, the bullet and shell has been busy in lessening our strength, for that is the way of war.

When in the trenches Bill and Kore amuse themselves by potting all day long at the German lines. A conversation like the following may be often heard.

Bill :—"Blimey, I see a 'ead."

Kore :—"Fire then." (Bill fires a shot.) "Got him?"

Bill :—"No blurry fear. The 'ead was a sandbag. I'll bet yer the shot they send back will come nearer me than you. Bet yer a copper."

Kore :—"Done." (A bullet whistles by on

the right of Bill's head. " I think they're firing at you."

Bill :—" Not me, matey, but you. It's their aiming that's bad. 'And over the coin." (Enter an officer.)

Officer :—" Don't keep your heads over the parapet, you'll get sniped. Keep under cover as much as possible."

Bill :—" Orl right, Sir."

Kore :—" Yes, sir." (Exit Officer.)

Bill :—" They say there's a war 'ere."

Kore :—" It's only a rumour."

At Cuinchy where the German trenches are hardly a hundred yards away from ours, the firing from the opposite trenches ceased for a moment and a voice called across.

" What about the Cup Final ? " It was then the finish of the English football season.

" Chelsea lost," said Bill, who was a staunch supporter of that team.

" Hard luck ! " came the answer from the German trench and firing was resumed. But Bill used his rifle no more until we changed into a new locality. " A blurry supporter of blurry Chelsea," he said. " 'E must be a damned good sort of sausage-eater, that feller. If ever I meet 'im in Lunnon after the war,

I'm goin' to make 'im as drunk as a public-'ouse fly."

"What are you going to do after the war?" I asked.

He rubbed his eyes which many sleepless nights in a shell-harried trench had made red and watery.

"What will I do?" he repeated. "I'll get two beds," he said, "and have a six months' snooze, and I'll sleep in one bed while the other's being made, matey."

In trench life many new friends are made and many old friendships renewed. We were nursing a contingent of Camerons, men new to the grind of trench work, and most of them hailing from Glasgow and the West of Scotland. On the morning of the second day one of them said to me, "Big Jock MacGregor wants to see you."

"Who's Big Jock?" I asked.

"He used to work on the railway at Greenock," I was told, and off I went to seek the man.

I found him eating bully beef and biscuit on the parapet. He was spotlessly clean, he had not yet stuck his spoon down the rim of his stocking where his skein should have been, he had a table knife and fork (things that we, old soldiers, had dispensed with ages ago), in short, he was a hat-box fellow, togged up to the nines, and as yet, green to the grind of war.

His age might be forty, he looked fifty, a fatherly sort of man, a real block of Caledonian Railway thrown, tartanised, into a trench.

" How are you, Jock ? " I said. I had never met him before.

" Are you Pat MacGill ? "

I nodded assent.

" Man, I've often heard of you, Pat," he went on, " I worked on the Sou' West, and my brother's an engine driver on the Caly. He reads your songs a'most every night. He says there are only two poets he'd give a fling for—that's you and Anderson, the man who wrote *Cuddle Doon*."

" How do you like the trenches, Jock ? "

" Not so bad, man, not so bad," he said.

" Killed any one yet ? " I asked.

" Not yet," he answered in all seriousness. " But there's a sniper over there," and he pointed a clean finger, quite untrenchy it was, towards the enemy's lines, " And he's fired three at me."

" At you ? " I asked.

" Ay, and I sent him five back ——"

" And didn't do him in ? " I asked.

" Not yet, but if I get another two or three at him, I'll not give much for his chance."

" Have you seen him ? " I asked, marvelling that Big Jock had already seen a sniper.

" No, but I heard the shots go off."

A rifle shot is the most deceptive thing in the world, so, like an old soldier wise in the work, I smiled under my hand.

I don't believe that Big Jock has killed his sniper yet, but it has been good to see him. When we meet he says, " What about the Caly, Pat ? " and I answer, " What about the Sou' West, Jock ? "

On the first Sunday after Trinity we marched out from another small village in the hot afternoon. This one was a model village, snug in the fields, and dwindling daily. The German shells are dropping there every day. In the course of another six months if the fronts of the contending armies do not change, that village will be a litter of red bricks and unpeopled ruins. As it is the women, children and old men still remain in the place and carry on their usual labours with the greatest fortitude and patience. The village children sell percussion caps of

German shells for half a franc each, but if the shell has killed any of the natives when it exploded, the cap will not be sold for less than thirty sous. But the sum is not too dear for a nose-cap with a history.

There are a number of soldiers buried in the graveyard of this place. At one corner four different crosses bear the following names: Anatole Séries, Private O'Shea, Corporal Smith and under the symbol of the Christian religion lies one who came from sunny heathen climes to help the Christian in his wars. His name is Jaighandthakur, a soldier of the Bengal Mountain Battery.

It was while here that Bill complained of the scanty allowance of his rations to an officer, when plum pudding was served at dinner.

"Me and Stoner 'as got 'ardly nuffink," Bill said.

"How much have you got?" asked the officer.

"You could 'ardly see it, it's so small," said Bill. "But now it's all gone."

"Gone?"

"A fly flew away with my portion, and Stoner's 'as fallen through the neck of 'is waterbottle," said Bill. The officer ordered both men to be served out with a second portion.

We left the village in the morning and marched for the best part of the day. We were going to hold a trench five kilometres north of Souchez and the Hills of Lorette. The trenches to which we were going had recently been held by the French but now that portion of the line is British; our soldiers fight side by side with the French on the Hills of Lorette at present.

The day was exceedingly hot, a day when men sweat and grumble as they march, when they fall down like dead things on the roadside at every halt and when they rise again they wonder how under Heaven they are going to drag their limbs and burdens along for the next forty minutes. We passed Les Brebes, like men in a dream, pursued a tortuous path across a wide field, in the middle of which are several shell-shattered huts and some acres of shell-scooped ground. The place was once held by a French battery and a spy gave the position away to the enemy. Early one morning the shells began to sweep in, carrying the message of death from guns miles away. Never have I seen such a memento of splendid gunnery, as that written large in shell-holes on that field.

The bomb-proof shelters are on a level with the ground, the vicinity is pitted as if with smallpox, but two hundred yards out on any side there is not a trace of a shell, every shot went true to the mark. A man with a rifle two hundred yards away could not be much more certain than the German gunners of a target as large. But their work went for nothing: the battery had changed its position the night previous to the attack. Had it remained there neither man nor gun would have escaped.

The communication trench we found to be one of the widest we had ever seen; a hand-barrow could have been wheeled along the floor. At several points the trench was roofed with heavy pit-props and sandbags proof against any shrapnel fire. It was an easy trench to march in, and we needed all the ease possible. The sweat poured from every pore, down our faces, our arms and legs, our packs seemed filled with lead, our haversacks rubbing against our hips felt like sand paper; the whole march was a nightmare. The water we carried got hot in our bottles and became almost undrinkable. In the reserve trench we got some tea, a godsend to us all.

We had just stepped into a long, dark, pit-prop-roofed tunnel and the light of the outer world made us blind. I shuffled up against a man who was sitting on one side, righted myself and stumbled against the knees of another who sat on a seat opposite.

"Will ye have a wee drop of tay, my man?" a voice asked, an Irish voice, a voice that breathed of the North of Ireland. I tried to see things, but could not. I rubbed my eyes and had a vision of an arm stretching towards me; a hand and a mess tin. I drank the tea greedily.

"There's a lot of you ones comin' up," the voice said. "You ones!" How often have I said "You ones," how often do I say it still when I'm too excited to be grammatical. "Ye had a' must to be too late for tay!" the voice said from the darkness.

"What does he say?" asked Pryor who was just ahead of me.

"He says that we were almost too late for tea," I replied and stared hard into the darkness on my left. Figures of men in khaki took form in the gloom, a bayonet sparkled; some one was putting a lid on a mess-tin and I could see the man doing it....

"Inniskillings?" I asked.

"That's us."

"Quiet?" I asked, alluding to their life in the trench.

"Not bad at all," was the answer. "A shell came this road an hour agone, and two of us got hit."

"Killed?"

"Boys, oh! boys, aye," was the answer; "and seven got wounded. Nine of the best, man, nine of the best. Have another drop of tay?"

At the exit of the tunnel the floor was covered with blood and the flies were buzzing over it; the sated insects rose lazily as we came up, settled down in front, rose again and flew back over our heads. What a feast they were having on the blood of men!

The trenches into which we had come were not so clean as many we had been in before; although the dug-outs were much better constructed than those in the British lines, they smelt vilely of something sickening and nauseous.

A week passed away and we were still in the trenches. Sometimes it rained, but for the most part the sky was clear and the sun very hot. The trenches were dug out of the chalk, the world in which we lived was a world of white and green, white parapet and parados with a fringe of grass on the superior slope of each. The place was very quiet, not more than two dozen shells came our way daily, and it was there that I saw a shell in air, the only shell in flight I have ever seen. It was dropping to earth behind the parados and I had a distinct view of the missile before ducking to avoid the splinters flung out by the explosion. Hundreds of shells have passed through the sky near me every day, I could almost see them by their sound and felt I could trace the line made by them in their flight, but this was the only time I ever saw one.

The hill land of Lorette stood up sullen on our right; in a basin scooped out on its face, a hollow not more than five hundred yards square we could see, night and day, an eternal artillery conflict in progress, in the daylight by the smoke and in the dark by the flashes of bursting shells. It was an awe-inspiring and wonderful picture this titanic struggle; when I looked on it, I felt that it was not good to see—it was the face of a god. The mortal who gazed on it must die. But by night and day I spent most of my spare time in watching the smoke of bursting shells and the flash of innumerable explosions.

One morning, after six days in the trenches, I was seated on the parados blowing up an air pillow which had been sent to me by an English friend and watching the fight up at Souchez when Bill came up to me.

" Wot's that yer've got ? " he asked.

" An air pillow," I answered.

" 'Ow much were yer rushed for it ? "

" Somebody sent it to me ," I said.

" To rest yer weary 'ead on ? "

I nodded.

" I like a fresh piller every night," said Bill.

" A fresh what ? "

" A fresh brick."

" How do you like these trenches ? " I asked after a short silence.

" Not much," he answered. " They're all blurry flies and chalk." He gazed ruefully at the white sandbags and an army ration of cheese rolled up in a paper on which blow-flies were congregating. Chalk was all over the place, the dug-outs were dug out of chalk, the sandbags were filled with chalk, every bullet, bomb and shell whirled showers of fine powdery chalk into the air, chalk frittered away from the parapets fell down into our mess-tins as we drank our tea, the rain-wet chalk melted to milk and whitened the barrels and actions of our rifles where they stood on the banquette, bayonets up to the sky.

Looking northward when one dared to raise his head over the parapet for a moment, could be seen white lines of chalk winding across a sea of green meadows splashed with daisies and scarlet poppies. Butterflies flitted from flower to flower and sometimes found their way into our trench where they rested for a moment on the chalk bags, only to rise again and vanish over the fringes of green that verged the limits of our world. Three miles away rising lonely over the beaten zone of emerald stood a red brick village, conspicuous by the spire of its church and an impudent chimney, with part of its side blown away, that stood stiff in the air. A miracle that it had not fallen to pieces. Over the latrine at the back the flies were busy, their buzzing reminded me of the sound made by shell splinters whizzing through the air.

The space between the trenches looked like a beautiful garden, green leaves hid all shrapnel scars on the shivered trees, thistles with magnificent blooms rose in line along the parapet, grasses hung over the sandbags of the parapet and seemed to be peering in at us asking if we would allow them to enter. The garden of death was a riot of colour, green, crimson, heliotrope and poppy-red. Even from amidst the chalk bags, a daring little flower could be seen showing its face; and a primrose came to blossom under the eaves of our dug-out. Nature was hard at work blotting out the disfigurement caused by man to the face of the country.

At noon I sat in the dug-out where Bill was busy repairing a defect in his mouth organ. The sun blazed overhead, and it was almost impossible to write, eat or even to sleep.

The dug-out was close and suffocating; the air stank of something putrid, of decaying flesh, of wasting bodies of French soldiers who had fallen in a charge and were now rotting in the midst of the fair poppy flowers. They lay as they fell, stricken headlong in the great frenzy of battle, their fingers wasted to the bone, still clasping their rifles or clenching the earth which they pulled from the ground in the mad agony of violent death. Now and again, mingled with the stench of death and decay, the breeze wafted into our dug-out an odour of flowers.

The order came like a bomb flung into the trench and woke us up like an electric thrill.

True we did not believe it at first, there are so many practical jokers in our ranks. Such an insane order! Had the head of affairs gone suddenly mad that such an order was issued. "All men get ready for a bath. Towels and soap are to be carried!!!"

"Where are we going to bathe?" I asked the platoon sergeant.

"In the village at the rear," he answered.

"There's nobody there, nothing but battered houses," I answered. "And the place gets shelled daily."

"That doesn't matter," said the platoon sergeant. "There's going to be a bath and a jolly good one for all. Hot water."

We went out to the village at the rear, the Village of Shattered Homes, which were bunched together under the wall of a rather pretentious villa that had so far suffered very little from the effects of the German artillery. As yet the roof and windows were all that were damaged, the roof was blown in and the window glass was smashed to pieces.

We got a good bath, a cold spray whizzed from the nozzle of a serpentine hose, and a share of underclothing. The last we needed badly for the chalk trenches were very verminous. We went back clean and wholesome, the bath put new life into us.

That same evening, what time the star-shells began to flare and the flashes of the guns could be seen on the hills of Lorette, two of our men got done to death in their dug-out. A shell hit the roof and smashed the pit-props down on top of the two soldiers. Death was instantaneous in both cases.

CHAPTER XVIII

The Covering Party

Along the road in the evening the brown battalions wind,
With the trenches threat of death before, the peaceful homes behind;
And luck is with you or luck is not, as the ticket of fate is drawn,
The boys go up to the trench at dusk, but who will come back at dawn?

THE darkness clung close to the ground, the spinney between our lines was a bulk of shadow thinning out near the stars. A light breeze scampered along the floor of the trench and seemed to be chasing something. The night was raw and making for rain; at midnight when my hour of guard came to an end I went to my dug-out, the spacious construction, roofed with long wooden beams heaped with sandbags, which was built by the French in the winter season, what time men were apt to erect substantial shelters, and know their worth. The platoon sergeant stopped me at the door.

"Going to have a kip, Pat?" he asked.

"If I'm lucky," I answered.

"Your luck's dead out," said the sergeant. "You're to be one of a covering party for the Engineers. They're out to-night repairing the wire entanglements."

"Any more of the Section going out?" I asked.

"Bill's on the job," I was told. The sergeant alluded to my mate, the vivacious Cockney, the spark who so often makes Section 3 in its dullest mood, explode with laughter.

Ten minutes later Bill and I, accompanied by a corporal and four other riflemen, clambered over the parapet out on to the open field. We came to the wire entanglements which ran along in front of the trench ten to fifteen yards away from the reverse slope of the parapet. The German artillery had played havoc with the wires some days prior to our occupation of the trench, the stakes had been battered down and most of the defence had been smashed to smithereens. Bombarding wire entanglements seems to be an artillery pastime; when we smash those of the Germans they reply by smashing ours, then both sides repair the damage only to start the game of demolition over again.

The line of entanglements does not run

parallel with the trench it covers, although when seen from the parapet its inner stakes seem always to be about the same distance away from the nearest sandbags. But taken in relation to the trench opposite the entanglements are laid with occasional V-shaped openings narrowing towards our trench.

The enemy plan an attack. At dusk or dawn their infantry will make a charge over the open ground, raked with machine gun, howitzer, and rifle fire. Between the trenches is the beaten zone, the field of death. The moment the attacking party pull down the sandbags from the parapet, its sole aim is to get to the other side. The men become creatures of instinct, mad animals with only one desire, that is to get to the other side where there is comparative safety. They dash up to a jumble of trip wires scattered broadcast over the field and thinning out to a point, the nearest point which they reach in the enemy's direction. Trip wires are the quicksands of the beaten zone, a man floundering amidst them gets lost. The attackers realize this and the instinct which tells them of a certain amount of safety in the vicinity of an unfriendly trench urges them pell mell into the V-shaped recess that narrows towards our lines. Here the attackers are heaped up, a target of wriggling humanity; ready prey for the concentrated fire of the rifles from the British trench. The narrow part of the V becomes a welter of concentrated horror, the attackers tear at the wires with their hands and get ripped flesh from bone, mutilated on the barbs in the frensied efforts to get through. The tragedy of an advance is painted red on the barbed wire entanglements.

In one point our wires had been cut clean through by a concussion shell and the entanglement looked as if it had been frozen into immobility in the midst of a riot of broken wires and shattered posts. We passed through the lane made by the shell and flopped flat to earth on the other side when a German star-shell came across to inspect us. The world between the trenches was lit up for a moment. The wires stood out clear in one glittering distortion, the spinney, full of dark racing shadows, wailed mournfully to the breeze that passed through its shrapnel-scarred branches, white as bone where their bark had been peeled away. In the mysteries of light and shade, in the threat that hangs forever over men in the trenches there was a wild fascination. I was for a moment tempted to rise up and shout across to the German trenches, I am here! No defiance would be in the shout. It was merely a momentary impulse born of adventure that intoxicates. Bill sprung to his feet suddenly, rubbing his face with a violent hand; this in full view of the enemy's trench in a light that illumined the place like a sun.

"Bill, Bill!" we muttered hoarsely.

"Well, blimey, that's a go," he said coughing and spitting. "What 'ave I done, splunk on a dead 'un I flopped, a stinking corpse. 'E was 'uggin' me, kissin' me. Oh! nark the game, ole stiff 'un," said Bill, addressing the ground where I could perceive a bundle of dark clothes, striped with red and deep in the grass. "Talk about rotten eggs burstin' on your jor; they're not in it."

The light of the star-shell waned and died away; the Corporal spoke to Bill.

"Next time a light goes up you be flat; your'e giving the whole damned show away," the Corporal said. "If you're spotted it's all up with us."

We fixed swords clamping them into the bayonet standards and lay flat on the ground in the midst of dead bodies of French soldiers.

Months before the French endeavoured to take the German trenches and got about half way across the field. There they stopped, mown down by rifle and machine gun fire and they lie there still, little bundles of wasting flesh in the midst of the poppies. When the star-shells went up I could see a face near me, a young face clean-shaven and very pale under a wealth of curly hair. It was the face of a mere boy, the eyes were closed as if the youth were only asleep. It looked as if the effacing finger of decay had forborne from working its will on the helpless thing. His hand still gripped the rifle, and the long bayonet on the standard shone when the light played upon it. It seemed as if he fell quietly to the ground, dead. Others, I could see, had died a death of agony; they lay there in distorted postures, some with faces battered out of recognition, others with their hands full of grass and clay as if they had torn up the earth in their mad, final frenzy. Not a nice bed to lie in during a night out on listening patrol.*

The Engineers were now at work just behind us, I could see their dark forms flitting amongst

* The London Irish charged over this ground later, and entered Loos on Saturday, 25th September, 1915.

the posts, straightening the old ones, driving in fresh supports and pulling the wires taut. They worked as quietly as possible, but to our ears, tensely strained, the noise of labour came like the rumble of artillery. The enemy must surely hear the sound. Doubtless he did, but probably his own working parties were busy just as ours were. In front when one of our star-shells went across I fancied that I could see dark forms standing motionless by the German trench. Perhaps my eyes played me false, the objects might be tree-trunks trimmed down by shell fire....

The message came out from our trench and the Corporal passed it along his party. "On the right a party of the —th London are working." This was to prevent us mistaking them for Germans. All night long operations are carried on between the lines, if daylight suddenly shot out about one in the morning what a scene would unfold itself in No Man's Land; listening patrols marching along, Engineers busy with the wires, sanitary squads burying the dead and covering parties keeping watch over all the workers.

"Halt! who goes there?"

The order loud and distinct came from the

vicinity of the German trench, then followed a mumbled reply and afterwards a scuffle a sound as of steel clashing in steel, and then subdued laughter. What had happened ? Next day we heard that a sergeant and three men of the —th were out on patrol and went too near the enemy's lines. Suddenly they were confronted by several dark forms with fixed bayonets and the usual sentry's challenge was yelled out in English. Believing that he had fallen across one of his own outposts, the unsuspecting sergeant gave the password for the night, approached those who challenged him and was immediately made prisoner. Two others met with the same fate, but one who had been lagging at the rear got away and managed to get back to his own lines. Many strange things happen between the lines at night ; working parties have no love for the place and hundreds get killed there.

The slightest tinge of dawn was in the sky when our party slipped back over the parapet and stood to arms on the banquette and yawned out the conventional hour when soldiers await the attacks which so often begin at dawn.

We go out often as working parties or listening patrols.

From Souchez to Ypres the firing line runs through a land of stinking drains, level fields, and shattered villages. We know those villages, we have lived in them, we have been sniped at in their streets and shelled in the houses. We have had men killed in them, blown to atoms or buried in masonry, done to death by some damnable instrument of war.

In our trenches near Souchez you can see the eternal artillery fighting on the hills of Lorette, up there men are flicked out of existence like flies in a hailstorm. The big straight road out of a village runs through our lines into the German trenches and beyond. The road is lined with poplars and green with grass; by day you can see the German sandbags from our trenches, by night you can hear the wind in the trees that bend towards one another as if in conversation. There is no whole house in the place; chimneys have been blown down and roofs are battered by shrapnel. But few of the people have gone away, they have become schooled in the process of accommodation, and accommodate themselves to a woeful change. They live with one foot on the top step of the cellar stairs, a shell sends them scampering down; they sleep there, they eat there, in their underground home they wait for the war to end. The men who are too old to fight labour in a neighbouring mine, which still does some work although its chimney is shattered and its coal waggons are scraps of wood and iron on broken rails. There are many graves by the church, graves of our boys, civilians' graves, children's graves, all victims of war. Children are there still, merry little kids with red lips and laughing eyes.

One day, when staying in the village, I met one, a dainty little dot, with golden hair and laughing eyes, a pink ribbon round a tress that hung roguishly over her left cheek. She smiled at me as she passed where I sat on the roadside under the poplars, her face was an angel's set in a disarray of gold. In her hand she carried an empty jug, almost as big as herself and she was going to her home, one of the inhabited houses nearest the fighting line. The day had been a very quiet one and the village took an opportunity to bask in the sun. I watched her go up the road tripping lightly on the grass, swinging her big jug. Life was a garland of flowers for her, it was good to watch her to see her trip along; the sight made me happy. What caused the German gunner, a simple woodman and a father himself perhaps, to fire at that moment? What demon guided the shell? Who can say? The shell dropped on the roadway just where the child was; I saw the explosion and dropped flat to avoid the splinters, when I looked again there was no child, no jug, where she had been was a heap of stones on the grass and dark curls of smoke rising up from it. I hastened indoors; the enemy were shelling the village again.

Our billet is a village with shell-scarred trees lining its streets, and grass peeping over its fallen masonry, a few inn signs still swing and look like corpses hanging; at night they creak as if in agony. This place was taken from the Germans by the French, from the French by the Germans and changed hands several times afterwards. The streets saw many desperate hand to hand encounters; they are clean now but the village stinks, men were buried there by cannon, they lie in the cellars with the wine barrels, bones, skulls, fleshless hands sticking up over the bricks; the grass has been busy in its endeavour to cloak up the horror, but it will take nature many years to hide the ravages of war.

In another small village three kilometres from the firing line I have seen the street so thick with flies that it was impossible to see the cobbles underneath. There we could get English papers the morning after publication: for penny papers we paid three halfpence, for halfpenny papers twopence! In a restaurant in the place we got a dinner consisting of vegetable soup, fried potatoes, and egg omelette, salad, bread, beer, a sweet and a cup of *café au lait* for fifteen sous per man. There too on a memorable occasion we were paid the sum of ten francs on pay day.

In a third village not far off six of us soldiers slept one night in a cellar with a man, his wife and seven children, one a sucking babe. That night the roof of the house was blown in by a shell. In the same place my mate and I went out to a restaurant for dinner, and a young Frenchman, a gunner, sat at our table. He came from the south, a shepherd boy from the foot hills of the Pyrenees. He shook hands with us, giving the left hand, the one next the heart, as a proof of comradeship when leaving. A shrapnel bullet caught him inside the door and he fell dead on the pavement. Every stone standing or fallen in the villages by the firing line has got a history, and a tragedy connected with it.

In some places the enemy's bullets search the main street by night and day; a journey from the rear to the trenches is made across the open, and the eternal German bullet never leaves off searching for our boys coming in to the firing line. You can rely on sandbagged safety in the villages, but on the way from there to the trenches you merely trust your luck; for the moment your life has gone out of your keeping.

No civilian is allowed to enter one place, but I have seen a woman there. We were coming in, a working party, from the trenches when the colour of dawn was in the sky. We met her on the street opposite the pile of bricks that once was a little church: the spire of the church was blown off months ago and it sticks point downwards in a grave. The woman was taken prisoner. Who was she? Where did she come from? None of us knew, but we concluded she was a spy. Afterwards we heard that she was a native who had returned to have a look at her home.

We were billeted at the rear of the village on the ground floor of a cottage. Behind our billet was the open country where Nature, the great mother, was busy; the butterflies flitted over the soldiers' graves, the grass grew over unburied dead men, who seemed to be sinking into the ground, apple trees threw out a wealth of blossom which the breezes flung broadcast to earth like young lives in the whirlwind of war. We first came to the place at midnight; in the morning when we got up we found outside our door, in the midst of a jumble of broken pump handles and biscuit tins, fragments of chairs, holy pictures, crucifixes and barbed wire entanglements, a dead dog dwindling to dust, the hair falling from its skin and the white bones showing. As we looked on the thing it moved, its belly heaved as if the animal had gulped in a mouthful of air. We stared aghast and our laughter was not hearty when a rat scurried out of the carcase and sought safety in a hole of the adjoining wall. The dog was buried by the Section 3. Four simple lines serve as its epitaph:—

Here lies a dog as dead as dead,
A Sniper's bullet through its head,
Untroubled now by shots and shells,
It rots and can do nothing else.

The village where I write this is shelled daily, yesterday three men, two women and two children, all civilians, were killed. The natives have become almost indifferent to shell-fire.

In the villages in the line of war between Souchez and Ypres strange things happen and wonderful sights can be seen.

CHAPTER XIX

Souvenir Hunters

I have a big French rifle, its stock is riddled clean,
And shrapnel smashed its barrel, likewise its magazine;
I've carried it from A to X and back to A again,
I've found it on the battlefield amidst the soldiers slain.
A souvenir for blighty away across the foam,
That's if the French authorities will let me take it home.

MOST people are souvenir hunters, but the craze for souvenirs has never affected me until now; at present I have a decent collection of curios, consisting amongst other things of a French rifle, which I took from the hands of a dead soldier on the field near Souchez; a little nickel boot, which was taken from the pack of a Breton piou-piou who was found dead by a trench in Vermelles—one of our men who obtained this relic carried it about with him for many weeks until he was killed by a shell and then the boot fell into my hands. I have two percussion caps, one from a shell that came through the roof of a dug-out and killed two of our boys, the other was gotten beside a dead lieutenant in a deserted house in

Festubert. In addition to these I have many shell splinters that fell into the trench and landed at my feet, rings made from aluminium timing-pieces of shells and several other odds and ends picked up from the field of battle. Once I found a splendid English revolver—but that is a story.

We were billeted in a model mining-village of red brick houses and terra cotta tiles, where every door is just like the one next to it and the whole place gives the impression of monotonous sameness relieved here and there by a shell-shattered roof, a symbol of sorrow and wanton destruction. In this place of an evening children may be seen out of doors listening for the coming of the German shells and counting the number that fall in the village. From our billets we went out to the trenches by Vermelles daily, and cut the grass from the trenches with reaping hooks. In the morning a white mist lay on the meadows and dry dung and dust rose from the roadway as we marched out to our labour.

We halted by the last house in the village, one that stood almost intact, although the adjoining buildings were well nigh levelled to the ground. My mate, Pryor, fixed his eyes on the villa.

"I'm going in there," he said pointing at the doors.

"Souvenirs?" I asked.

"Souvenirs," he replied.

The two of us slipped away from the platoon and entered the building. On the ground floor stood a table on which a dinner was laid; an active service dinner of soup made from soup tablets (2*d.* each) the wrappers of which lay on the tiled floor, some tins of bully beef, opened, a loaf, half a dozen apples and an unopened tin of *café au lait.* The dinner was laid for four, although there were only three forks, two spoons and two clasp knives, the latter were undoubtedly used to replace table knives. Pryor looked under the table, then turned round and fixed a pair of scared eyes on me, and beckoned to me to approach. I came to his side and saw under the table on the floor a human hand, severed from the arm at the wrist. Beside it lay a web-equipment, torn to shreds, a broken range-finder and a Webley revolver, long of barrel and heavy of magazine.

"A souvenir," said Pryor. "It must have been some time since that dinner was made; the bully smells like anything."

"The shell came in there," I said pointing at

the window, the side of which was broken a little, "and it hit one poor beggar anyway. Nobody seems to have come in here since then."

"We'll hide the revolver," Pryor remarked, "and we'll come here for it to-night."

We hid the revolver behind the door in a little cupboard in the wall; we came back for it two days later, but the weapon was gone though the hand still lay on the floor. What was the history of that house and of the officers who sat down to dinner? Will the tragedy ever be told?

I had an interesting experience near Souchez when our regiment was holding part of the line in that locality. On the way in was a single house, a red brick villa, standing by the side of the communication trench which I used to pass daily when I went out to get water from the carts at the rear. One afternoon I climbed over the side and entered the house by a side door that looked over the German lines. The building was a conspicuous target for the enemy, but strange to say, it had never been touched by shell fire; now and again bullets peppered the walls, chipped the bricks and smashed the window-panes. On the ground floor was a large living-room with a big-bodied stove in the centre of the floor, religious pictures hung on the wall, a grandfather's clock stood in the niche near the door, the blinds were drawn across the shattered windows, and several chairs were placed round a big table near the stove. Upstairs in the bedrooms the beds were made and in one apartment a large perambulator, with a doll flung carelessly on its coverlet, stood near the wall, the paper of which was designed in little circles and in each circle were figures of little boys and girls, hundreds of them, frivolous mites, absurd and gay.

Another stair led up to the garret, a gloomy place bare under the red tiles, some of which were broken. Looking out through the aperture in the roof I could see the British and German trenches drawn as if in chalk on a slate of green by an erratic hand, the hand of an idle child. Behind the German trenches stood the red brick village of ——, with an impudent chimney standing smokeless in the air, and a burning mine that vomited clouds of thick black smoke over meadow-fields splashed with poppies. Shells were bursting everywhere over the grass and the white lines; the greenish grey fumes of lyddite, the white smoke of shrapnel rose into mid-air, curled away and died. On the left of the village a road ran back into the enemy's land, and from it a cloud of dust was rising over the tree-tops; no doubt vehicles of war which I could not see were moving about in that direction. I stayed up in that garret for quite an hour full of the romance of my watch and when I left I took my souvenir with me, a picture of the Blessed Virgin in a cedar frame. That night we placed it outside our dug-out over the door. In the morning we found it smashed to pieces by a bullet.

Daily I spent some time in the garret on my way out to the water-cart; and one day I found it occupied. Five soldiers and an officer were standing at my peephole when I got up, with a large telescope fixed on a tripod and trained on the enemy's lines. The War Intelligence Department had taken over the house for an observation post.

"What do you want here?" asked the officer.

Soldiers are ordered to keep to the trenches on the way out and in, none of the houses that line the way are to be visited. It was a case for a slight prevarication. My water jar was out in the trench: I carried my rifle and a bandolier.

" I'm looking for a sniping position," I said.

" You cannot stop here," said the officer. " We've taken this place over. Try some of the houses on the left."

I cleared out. Three days later when on my usual errand I saw that the roof of my observation villa had been blown in. Nobody would be in there now I concluded and ventured inside. The door which stood at the bottom of the garret stair was closed. I caught hold of the latch and pulled it towards me. The door held tight. As I struggled with it I had a sense of pulling against a detaining hand that strove to hide a mystery, something fearful, from my eye. It swung towards me slowly and a pile of bricks fell on my feet as it opened. Something dark and liquid oozed out under my boots. I felt myself slip on it and knew that I stood on blood. All the way up the rubble-covered stairs there was blood, it had splashed red on the railings and walls. Laths, plaster, tiles and beams lay on the floor above and in the midst of the jumble was a shattered telescope still moist with the blood of men. Had all been killed and were all those I had met a few days before in the garret when the shell landed on the roof? It was impossible to tell.

I returned to the dug-out meditating on the strange things that can be seen by him who goes souvenir-hunting between Souchez and Ypres. As I entered I found Bill gazing mutely at some black liquid in a sooty mess-tin.

" Some milk, Bill," I said handing him the tin of Nestle's which had just come to me in a Gargantuan parcel from an English friend.

" No milk, matey," he answered, " I'm feelin' done up proper, I am. Cannot eat a bite. Tummy out of order, my 'ead spinnin' like a top. When's sick parade ? " he asked.

" Seven o'clock," I said, " Is it as bad as that ? "

" Worse than that," he answered with a smile, " 'Ave yer a cigarette to spare ? "

" Yes," I answered, fumbling in my pocket.

" Well, give it to somebody as 'asn't got none," said Bill, " I'm off the smokin' a bit."

The case was really serious since Bill could not smoke, a smokeless hour was for him a Purgatorial period, his favourite friend was his fag. After tea I went with him to the dressing station, and Ted Vittle of Section 4 accompanied us. Ted's tummy was also out of order and his head was spinning like a top. The men's equipment was carried out, men going sick from the trenches to the dressing-station at the rear carry their rifles and all portable property in case they are sent off to hospital. The sick soldier's stuff always goes to hospital with him.

I stood outside the door of the dressing-station while the two men were in with the M.O. "What's wrong, Bill?" I asked when he came out.

"My tempratoor's an 'undred and nine," said my comrade.

"A hundred and what?" I ejaculated.

"'Undred point nine 'is was," said Ted Vittle. "Mine's a 'undred point eight. The Twentieth 'as 'ad lots of men gone off to 'orsp to-day sufferin' from the same thing. Pyraxis the M.O. calls it. Trench fever is the right name."

"Right?" interrogated Bill.

"Well it's a name we can understand," said Ted.

"Are you going back to the trenches again?" I asked.

"We're to sleep 'ere to-night in the cellar under the dressin'-station," they told me. "In the mornin' we're to report to the doctor again. 'E's a bloke 'e is, that doctor. 'E says we're to take nothing but heggs and milk and the milk must be boiled."

"Is the army going to supply it?"

"No blurry fear," said Bill. "Even if we 'ad the brass and the appetite we can't buy any milk or heggs 'ere."

I went back to the firing trench alone. Bill and Ted Vittle did not return the next day or the day after. Three weeks later Bill came back.

We were sitting in our dug-out at a village the bawl of a donkey from Souchez, when a jew's harp, playing ragtime was heard outside.

"Bill," we exclaimed in a voice, and sure enough it was Bill back to us again, trig and tidy from hospital, in a new uniform, new boots and with that air of importance which can only be the privilege of a man who has seen strange sights in strange regions.

"What's your temperature?" asked Stoner.

"Blimey, it's the correct thing now, but it didn't arf go up and down," said Bill sitting down on the dug-out chair, our only one since a shell dropped through the roof. Some days before B Company had held the dug-out and two of the boys were killed. "It's no fun the 'orspital I can tell yer."

"What sort of disease is Pyraxis?" asked Goliath.

It's not 'arf bad, if you've got it bad, and it's not good when you've it only 'arf bad," said Bill, adding, "I mean that if I 'ad it bad I would get off to blighty, but my case was only a light one, not so bad as Ted Vittle. 'E's not back yet, maybe it's a trip across the Channel for 'im. 'E was real bad when 'e walked down with me to Mazingarbe. I was rotten too, couldn't smoke. It was sit down and rest for fifteen minutes then walk for five. Mazingarbe is only a mile and an 'arf from the dressing-station and it took us three hours to get down; from there we took the motor-ambulance to the clearing hospital. There was a 'ot bath there and we were put to bed in a big 'ouse, blankets, plenty of them and a good bed. 'Twas a grand place to kip in. Bad as I was, I noticed that."

"No stand-to at dawn?" I said.

"Two 'ours before dawn we 'ad to stand-to in our blankets, matey," said Bill. "The Germans began to shell the blurry place and 'twas up to us to 'op it. We went dozens of us to the rear in a 'bus. Shook us! We were rattled about like tins on cats' tails and dumped down at another 'orsp about breakfast time.

My tempratoor was up more than ever there; I almost burst the thremometur. And Ted! Blimey, yer should 'ave seen Ted! Lost to the wide, 'e was. 'E could 'ardly speak; but 'e managed to give me his mother's address and I was to write 'ome a long letter to 'er when 'e went West."

"Allowed to 'ave peace in that place! No fear; the Boches began to shell us, and they sent over fifty shells in 'arf an 'our. All troops were ordered to leave the town and we went with the rest to a 'orsp under canvas in X——

"A nice quiet place X—— was, me and Ted was along with two others in a bell-tent and 'ere we began to get better. Our clothes were taken from us, all my stuff and two packets of fags and put into a locker. I don't know what I was thinking of when I let the fags go. There was one feller as had two francs in his trousers' pocket when 'e gave 'is trousers in and 'e got the wrong trousers back. 'E discovered that one day when 'e was goin' to send the R.A.M.C. orderly out for beer for all 'ands.

"'Twas a 'ungry place X. We were eight days in bed and all we got was milk and once or twice a hegg. Damned little heggs they were; they must 'ave been laid by tomtits in a 'urry. I got into trouble once; I climbed up the tent-pole one night just to 'ave a song on my own, and when I was on the top down comes the whole thing and I landed on Ted Vittle's bread basket. 'Is tempratoor was up to a 'undred and one point five next mornin'. The doctor didn't 'arf give me a look when 'e 'eard about me bein' up the pole."

"Was he a nice fellow, the doctor?" I asked.

"Not 'arf, 'e wasn't," said Bill. "When I got into my old uniform 'e looked 'ard at my cap. You remember it boys; 'twas more like a ragman's than a soldier of the King's. Then 'e arst me: ''Ave yer seen much war?' 'Not 'arf, I 'avent,' I told him. 'I thought so,' 'e said, 'judgin' by yer cap.' And 'e told the orderly to indent me for a brand new uniform. And 'e gave me two francs to get a drink when I was leavin'."

"Soft-hearted fellow," said Goliath.

"Was he!" remarked Bill. "Yer should be there when 'e came in one mornin'."

"'Ow d'ye feel?" he asked Ted Vittle.

"Not fit at all, sir," says Ted.

"Well, carry on," said the doctor.

I looked at Ted, Ted looked at me and 'e tipped me the wink.

" 'Ow d'ye feel," said the doctor to me.

" Not fit at all," I answers.

" Back to duties," 'e said and my jaw dropped with a click like a rifle bolt. 'Twas ten minutes after that when 'e gave me the two francs."

" I saw Spud 'Iggles, 'im that was wounded at Givenchy ; " Bill informed us after he had lit a fresh cigarette.

" 'Ole Spud ! "

" 'Ows Spud ? "

" Not so bad, yer know," said Bill, answering our last question. " 'E's got a job."

" A good one ? " I queried.

" Not 'arf," Bill said. " 'E goes round with the motor car that goes to places where soldiers are billeted and gathers up all the ammunition, bully beef tins, tins of biscuits and everything worth anything that's left behind —"

" Bill Teake. Is Bill Teake there ? " asked a corporal at the door of the dug-out.

" I'm 'ere, old Sawbones," said Bill, " wot d'ye want me for ? "

" It's your turn on sentry," said the corporal.

" Oh ! blimey, that's done it ! " grumbled

Bill. "I feel my tempratoor goin' up again. It's always some damn fatigue or another in this cursed place. I wonder when will I 'ave the luck to go sick again."

CHAPTER XX

The Women of France

Lonely and still the village lies,
The houses asleep and the blinds all drawn.
The road is straight as the bullet flies,
And the east is touched with the tinge of dawn.

Shadowy forms creep through the night,
Where the coal-stacks loom in their ghostly lair;
A sentry's challenge, a spurt of light,
A scream as a woman's soul takes flight
Through the quivering morning air.

WE had been working all morning in a cornfield near an *estaminet* on the La Bassée Road. The morning was very hot, and Pryor and I felt very dry; in fact, when our corporal stole off on the heels of a sergeant who stole off, we stole off to sin with our superiors by drinking white wine in an *estaminet* by the La Bassée Road.

"This is not the place to dig trenches," said the sergeant when we entered.

"We're just going to draw out the plans of the new traverse," Pryor explained. "It is to be made on a new principle, and a rifleman on sentry-go can sleep there and get wind of the approach of a sergeant by the vibration of stripes rubbing against the walls of the trench."

"Every man in the battalion must not be in here," said the sergeant looking at the khaki crowd and the full glasses. "I can't allow it and the back room empty."

Pryor and I took the hint and went to the low roofed room in the rear, where we found two persons, a woman and a man. The woman was sweating over a stove, frying cutlets and the man was sitting on the floor peeling potatoes into a large bucket. He was a thick-set lump of a fellow, with long, hairy arms, dark heavy eyebrows set firm over sharp, inquisitive eyes, a snub nose, and a long scar stretching from the butt of the left ear up to the cheek-bone. He wore a nondescript pair of loose baggy trousers, a fragment of a shirt and a pair of bedroom slippers. He peeled the potatoes with a knife, a long rapier-like instrument which he handled with marvellous dexterity.

"Digging trenches?" he asked, hurling a potato into the bucket.

I understand French spoken slowly, Pryor, who was educated in Paris, speaks French and he told the potato-peeler that we had been at work since five o'clock that morning.

"The Germans will never get back here again unless as prisoners."

"They might thrust us back; one never knows," said Pryor.

"Thrust us back! Never!" The potato swept into the bucket with a whizz like a spent bullet. "Their day has come! Why? Because they're beaten, our 75 has beaten them. That's it: the 75, the little love. Pip! pip! pip! pip! Four little imps in the air one behind the other. Nothing can stand them. Bomb! one lands in the German trench. *Plusieurs morts, plusieurs blessés.* Run! Some go right, some left. The second shot lands on the right, the third on the left, the fourth finishes the job. The dead are many; other guns are good, but none so good as the 75."

"What about the gun that sent this over?"

Pryor, as he spoke, pointed at the percussion cap of one of the gigantic shells with which the Germans raked La Bassée Road in the early stages of the war, what time the enemy's enthusiasm for destruction had not the nice discrimination that permeates it now. A light shrapnel shell is more deadly to a marching platoon than the biggest "Jack Johnson." The shell relic before us, the remnant of a mammoth Krupp design, was cast off by a shell in the field heavy with ripening corn and rye, opposite the doorway. When peace breaks out, and holidays to the scene of the great war become fashionable, the woman of the *estaminet* is going to sell the percussion cap to the highest bidder. There are many mementos of the great fight awaiting the tourists who come this way with a long purse, "après la guerre." At present a needy urchin will sell the nose-cap of a shell, which has killed multitudes of men and horses, for a few sous. Officers, going home on leave, deal largely with needy French urchins who live near the firing line.

"A great gun, the one that sent that," said the Frenchman, digging the clay from the eye of a potato and looking at the percussion-cap which lay on the mantelpiece under a picture of the Virgin and Child. "But compared with the 75, it is nothing; no good. The big shell comes boom! It's in no hurry. You hear it and you're into your dug-out before it arrives. It is like thunder, which you hear and you're in shelter when the rain comes. But the 75, it is lightning. It comes silently, it's quicker than its own sound."

"Do you work here?" asked Pryor.

"I work here," said the potato-peeler.

"In a coal-mine?"

"Not in a coal-mine," was the answer. "I peel potatoes."

"Always?"

"Sometimes," said the man. "I'm out from the trenches on leave for seven days. First time since last August. Got back from Souchez to-day."

"Oh!" I ejaculated.

"Oh!" said Pryor. "Seen some fighting?"

"Not much," said the man, "not too much." His eyes lit up as with fire and he sent a potato stripped clean of its jacket up to the roof but with such precision that it dropped down straight into the bucket. "First we went south and the Germans came across up north. 'Twas turn about and up like mad; perched on taxis, limbers, ambulance waggons, anything. We got into battle near Paris. The Boches came in clusters, they covered the ground like flies on the dead at Souchez. The 75's came into work there. 'Twas wonderful. Pip! pip! pip! pip! Men were cut down, wiped out in hundreds. When the gun was useless—guns had short lives and glorious lives there—

a new one came into play and killed, killed, until it could stand the strain no longer."

"Much hand-to-hand fighting?" asked Pryor.

"The bayonet! Yes!" The potato-peeler thrust his knife through a potato and slit it in two. "The Germans said 'Eugh! Eugh! Eugh!' when we went for them like this." He made several vicious prods at an imaginary enemy. "And we cut them down."

He paused as if at a loss for words, and sent his knife whirling into the air where it spun at an alarming rate. I edged my chair nearer the door, but the potato-peeler, suddenly standing upright, caught the weapon by the haft as it circled and bent to lift a fresh potato.

"What is that for?" asked Pryor, pointing to a sword wreathed in a garland of flowers, tattooed on the man's arm.

"The rapier," said the potato-peeler. "I'm a fencer, a master-fencer; fenced in Paris and several places."

The woman of the house, the man's wife, had been buzzing round like a bee, droning out in an incoherent voice as she served the customers. Now she came up to the master-fencer, looked at him in the face for a second, and then looked at the bucket. The sweat oozed from her face like water from a sponge.

"Hurry, and get the work done," she said to her husband, then she turned to us. "You're keeping him from work," she stuttered, "you two, chattering like parrots. Allez-vous en! Allez-vous en!"

We left the house of the potato-peeler and returned to our digging. The women of France are indeed wonderful.

That evening Bill came up to me as I was sitting on the banquette. In his hand was an English paper that I had just been reading and in his eye was wrath.

"The 'ole geeser's fyce is in this 'ere thing again," he said scornfully. "Blimy! it's like the bad weather, it's everywhere."

"Whose face do you refer to?" I asked my friend.

"This Jimace," was the answer and Bill pointed to the photo of a well-known society lady who was shown in the act of escorting a wounded soldier along a broad avenue of trees that tapered away to a point where an English country mansion showed like a doll's house in the distance. "Every pyper I open she's in it; if she's not makin' socks for poor Tommies at the front, she's tyin' bandages on wounded Tommies at 'ome."

"There's nothing wrong in that," I said, noting the sarcasm in Bill's voice.

"S'pose its natural for 'er to let everybody know what she does, like a 'en that lays a negg," my mate answered. "She's on this pyper or that pyper every day. She's learnin' nursin' one day, learnin' to drive an ambulance the next day, she doesn't carry a powder puff in 'er vanity bag at present ——"

"Who said so?" I asked.

"It's 'ere in black and white," said Bill. "'Er vanity bag 'as given place to a respirator, an' instead of a powder puff she now carries an antiskeptic bandage. It makes me sick; it's all the same with women in England. 'Ere's another picture called 'Bathin' as usual.' A dozen of girls out in the sea (jolly good legs some of 'em 'as, too) 'avin' a bit of a frisky. Listen what it says: 'Despite the trying times the English girls are keepin' a brave 'eart ——' Oh! 'ang it, Pat, they're nothin' to the French girls, them birds at 'ome."

"What about that girl you knew at St. Albans?" I asked. "You remember how she slid down the banisters and made toffee."

"She wasn't no class, you know," said Bill.

"She never answered the verse you sent from Givenchy, I suppose," I remarked.

"It's not that——"

"Did she answer your letter saying she reciprocated your sentiments?" I asked.

"Reshiperate your grandmother, Pat!" roared Bill. "Nark that language, I say. Speak that I can understand you. Wait a minute till I reshiperate that," he suddenly exclaimed pressing a charge into his rifle magazine and curving over the parapet. He sent five shots in the direction from which he supposed the sniper who had been potting at us all day, was firing. Then he returned to his argument.

"You've seen that bird at the farm in Mazingarbe?" he asked.

"Yes," I replied. "Pryor said that her ankles were abnormally thick."

"Pryor's a fool," Bill exclaimed.

"But they really looked thick——"

"You're a bigger fool than 'im!"

"I didn't know you had fallen in love with the girl," I said. "How did it happen?"

"Blimey, I'm not in love," said my mate, "but I like a girl with a good 'eart. 'Twas out in the horchard in the farm I first met 'er. I was out pullin' apples, pinchin' them if you like to say so, and I was shakin' the apples from the branches. I had to keep my eyes on the farm to see that nobody seen me while I shook. It takes a devil of a lot of strength to rumble apples off a tree when you're shakin' a trunk that's stouter than the bread basket of a Bow butcher. All at once I saw the girl of the farm comin' runnin' at me with a stick. Round to the other side of the tree I ran like lightnin', and after me she comes. Then round to the other side went I ——"

"Which side?" I asked.

"The side she wasn't on," said Bill. "After me she came and round to her side I 'opped——"

"Who was on the other side now?" I inquired.

"I took good care that she was always on the other side until I saw what she was up to with the stick," said Bill. "But d'yer know what the stick was for? 'Twas to help me to bring down the apples. Savve. They're great women, the women of France," concluded my mate.

The women of France! what heroism and fortitude animates them in every shell-shattered village from Souchez to the sea! What labours they do in the fields between the foothills of the Pyrenees and the Church of ——, where the woman nearest the German lines sells rum under the ruined altar! The plough and sickle are symbols of peace and power in the hands of the women of France in a land where men destroy and women build. The young girls of the hundred and one villages which fringe the line of destruction, proceed with their day's work under shell fire, calm as if death did not wait ready to pounce on them at every corner.

I have seen a woman in one place take her white horse from the pasture when shells were falling in the field and lead the animal out again when the row was over; two of her neighbours were killed in the same field the day before. One of our men spoke to her and pointed out that the action was fraught with danger. "I am convinced of that," she replied. "It is madness to remain here," she was told, and she asked "Where can I go to?" During the winter the French occupied the trenches nearer her home; her husband fought there, but the French have gone further south now and our men occupy their place in dug-out and trench but not in the woman's heart. "The English soldiers have come and my husband had to go away," she says. "He went south beyond Souchez, and now he's dead."

The woman, we learned, used to visit her husband in his dug-out and bring him coffee for breakfast and soup for dinner; this in winter when the slush in the trenches reached the waist and when soldiers were carried out daily suffering from frostbite.

A woman sells *café noir* near Cuinchy Brewery in a jumble of bricks that was once her home. Once it was *café au lait* and it cost four sous a cup, she only charges three sous now since her cow got shot in the stomach outside her ramshackle *estaminet*. Along with a few mates I was in the place two months ago and a bullet entered the door and smashed the coffee pot; the woman now makes coffee in a biscuit tin.

The road from our billet to the firing line is as uncomfortable as a road under shell fire can be, but what time we went that way nightly as working parties, we met scores of women carrying furniture away from a deserted village behind the trenches. The French military authorities forbade civilians to live there and drove them back to villages that were free from danger. But nightly they came back, contrary to orders, and carried away property to their temporary homes. Sometimes, I suppose they took goods that were not entirely their own, but at what risk! One or two got killed nightly and many were wounded. However, they still persisted in coming back and carrying away beds, tables, mirrors and chairs in all sorts of queer conveyances, barrows, perambulators and light spring-carts drawn by strong intelligent dogs.

"They are great women, the women of France," as Bill Teake remarks.

CHAPTER XXI

IN THE WATCHES OF THE NIGHT

"What do you do with your rifle, son?" I clean it every day,
And rub it with an oily rag to keep the rust away;
I slope, present and port the thing when sweating on parade.
I strop my razor on the sling; the bayonet stand is made
For me to hang my mirror on. I often use it, tòo,
As handle for the dixie, sir, and lug around the stew.
"But did you ever fire it, son?" Just once, but never more.
I fired it at a German trench, and when my work was o'er
The sergeant down the barrel glanced, and looked at me and said,
"Your hipe is dirty, sloppy Jim; an extra hour's parade!"

THE hour was midnight. Over me and about me was the wonderful French summer night; the darkness, blue and transparent, splashed with star-shells, hung around me and gathered itself into a dark streak on the floor of the trench beneath the banquette on which I stood. Away on my right were the Hills ot Lorette, Souchez, and the Labyrinth where big guns eternally spoke, and where the searchlights now touched the heights with long tremulous white arms. To my left the star-shells rose and fell in brilliant riot above the battle-line that disfigured the green meadows between my trench and Ypres, and out on my front a thousand yards away were the German trenches with the dead wasting to clay amid the poppy-flowers in the spaces between. The dug-out, in which my mates rested and dreamt, lay silent in the dun shadows of the parados.

Suddenly a candle was lit inside the door, and I could see our corporal throw aside the overcoat that served as blanket and place the tip of a cigarette against the spluttering flame. Bill slept beside the corporal's bed, his head on a bully beef tin, and one naked arm, sunned and soiled to a khaki tint, lying slack along the earthen floor. The corporal came out puffing little curls of smoke into the night air.

" Quiet ? " he asked.

" Dull enough, here," I answered. " But there's no peace up by Souchez."

" So I can hear," he answered, flicking the ash from his cigarette and gazing towards the hills where the artillery duel was raging. " Have the working parties come up yet ? " he asked.

" Not yet," I answered, " but I think I hear men coming now."

They came along the trench, about two hundred strong, engineers and infantry, men carrying rifles, spades, coils of barbed wire, wooden supports, &c. They were going out digging on a new sap and putting up fresh wire entanglements. This work, when finished, would bring our fire trench three hundred yards nearer the enemy. Needless to say, the Germans were engaged on similar work, and they were digging out towards our lines.

The working party came to a halt; and one of them sat down on the banquette at my feet, asked for a match and lit a cigarette.

"You're in the village at the rear?" I said.

"We're reserves there," he answered. "It's always working-parties; at night and at day. Sweeping gutters and picking papers and bits of stew from the street. Is it quiet here?"

"Very quiet," I answered. "We've only had five killed and nine wounded in six days. How is your regiment getting along?"

"Oh, not so bad," said the man; "some go west at times, but it's what one has to expect out here."

The working party were edging off, and some of the men were clambering over the parapet.

"Hi! Ginger!" someone said in a loud

whisper, " Ginger Weeson; come along at once ! "

The man on the banquette got to his feet, put out his cigarette and placed the fag-end in his cartridge pouch. He would smoke this when he returned, on the neutral ground between the lines a lighted cigarette would mean death to the smoker. I gave Ginger Weeson a leg over the parapet and handed him his spade when he got to the other side. My hour on sentry-go was now up and I went into my dug-out and was immediately asleep.

I was called again at one, three-quarters of an hour later.

" What's up ? " I asked the corporal who wakened me.

" Oh, there's a party going down to the rear for rations," I was told. " So you've got to take up sentry-go till stand-to ; that'll be for an hour or so. You're better out in the air now for its beginning to stink everywhere, but the dug-out is the worst place of all."

So saying, the corporal entered the dug-out and stretched himself on the floor ; he was going to have a sleep despite his mean opinion of the shelter.

The stench gathers itself in the early morning ;

in that chill hour which precedes the dawn one can almost see the smell ooze from the earth of the firing line. It is penetrating, sharp, and well-nigh tangible, the odour of herbs, flowers, and the dawn mixed with the stench of rotting meat and of the dead. You can taste it as it enters your mouth and nostrils, it comes in slowly, you feel it crawl up your nose and sink with a nauseous slowness down the back of the throat through the windpipe and into the stomach.

I leant my arms on the sandbags and looked across the field; I fancied I could see men moving in the darkness, but when the star-shells went up there was no sign of movement out by the web of barbed-wire entanglements. The new sap with its bags of earth stretched out chalky white towards the enemy; the sap was not more than three feet deep yet, it afforded very little protection from fire. Suddenly rising eerie from the space between the lines, I heard a cry. A harrowing "Oh!" wrung from a tortured soul, then a second "Oh!" ear-splitting, deafening. Something must have happened, one of the working party was hit I knew. A third "Oh!" followed, weak it was and infantile, then intense silence wrapped up everything as in a cloak. But only for a moment. The enemy must have heard the cry for a dozen star-shells shot towards us and frittered away in sparks by our barbed-wire entanglements. There followed a second of darkness and then an explosion right over the sap. The enemy were firing shrapnel shells on the working party. Three, four shells exploded simultaneously out in front. I saw dark forms rise up and come rushing into shelter. There was a crunching, a stumbling and a gasping as if for air. Boots struck against the barbed entanglements, and like trodden mice, the wires squeaked in protest. I saw a man, outlined in black against the glow of a starshell, struggling madly as he endeavoured to loose his clothing from the barbs on which it caught. There was a ripping and tearing of tunics and trousers....A shell burst over the men again and I saw two fall; one got up and clung to the arm of a mate, the other man crawled on his belly towards the parapet.

In their haste they fell over the parapet into the trench, several of them. Many had gone back by the sap, I could see them racing along crouching as they ran. Out in front several forms were bending over the ground attending to the wounded. From my left the message came "Stretcher-bearers at the double." And I passed it along.

Two men who had scrambled over the parapet were sitting on my banquette, one with a scratched forehead, the other with a bleeding finger. Their mates were attending to them binding up the wounds.

"Many hurt?" I asked.

"A lot 'ave copped a packet," said the man with the bleeding finger.

"We never 'eard the blurry things come, did we?" he asked his mates.

"Never 'eard nothin', we didn't till the thing burst over us," said a voice from the trench. "I was busy with Ginger ——"

"Ginger Weeson?" I enquired.

"That's 'im," was the reply. "Did yer 'ear 'im yell? Course yer did; ye'd 'ave 'eard 'im over at La Bassée."

"What happened to him?" I asked.

"A bullet through 'is belly," said the voice. "When 'e roared I put my 'and on 'is mouth and 'e gave me such a punch. I was nearly angry, and 'im in orful pain. Pore Ginger! Not many get better from a wound like his one."

Their wounds dressed, the men went away; others came by carrying out the stricken; many had fractured limbs, one was struck on the shoulder, another in the leg and one I noticed had several teeth knocked away.

The working-party had one killed and fifty-nine wounded in the morning's work; some of the wounded, amongst them, Ginger Weeson, died in hospital.

The ration-party came back at two o'clock jubilant. The post arrived when the men were in the village and many bulky parcels came in for us. Meals are a treat when parcels are bulky. We would have a fine breakfast.

CHAPTER XXII

ROMANCE

The young recruit is apt to think
  Of war as a romance;
But he'll find its boots and bayonets
  When he's somewhere out in France.

WHEN the young soldier takes the long, poplar-lined road from —— his heart is stirred with the romance of his mission. It is morning and he is bound for the trenches; the early sunshine is tangled in the branches, and silvery gossamer, beaded with iridescent jewels of dew, hang fairylike from the green leaves. Birds are singing, crickets are thridding in the grass and the air is full of the minute clamouring, murmuring and infinitesimal shouting of little living things. Cool, mysterious shadows are cast like intricate black lace upon the roadway, light is reflected from the cobbles in the open spaces, and on, on, ever so far on, the white road runs straight as an arrow into the land of mystery, the Unknown.

In front is the fighting line, where trench after trench, wayward as rivers, wind discreetly through meadow and village. By day you can mark it by whirling lyddite fumes rising from the ground, and puffs of smoke curling in the air ; at night it is a flare of star-shells and lurid flamed explosions colouring the sky line with the lights of death.

Under the moon and stars, the line of battle, seen from a distance, is a red horizon, ominous and threatening, fringing a land of broken homes, ruined villages, and blazing funeral pyres. There the mirth of yesteryear lives only in a soldier's dreams, and the harvest of last autumn rots with withering men on the field of death and decay.

Nature is busy through it all, the grasses grow green over the dead, and poppies fringe the parapets where the bayonets glisten, the sky-larks sing their songs at dawn between the lines, the frogs chuckle in the ponds at dusk, the grasshoppers chirrup in the dells where the wild iris, jewel-starred, bends mournfully to the breezes of night. In it all, the watching, the waiting, and the warring, is the mystery, the enchantment, and the glamour of romance ; and romance is dear to the heart of the young soldier.

I have looked towards the horizon when the sky was red-rimmed with the lingering sunset of midsummer and seen the artillery rip the heavens with spears of flame, seen the star-shells burst into fire and drop showers of slittering sparks to earth, seen the pale mists of evening rise over black, mysterious villages, woods, houses, gun-emplacements, and flat meadows, blue in the evening haze.

Aeroplanes flew in the air, little brown specks, heeling at times and catching the sheen of the setting sun, when they glimmered like flame. Above, about, and beneath them were the white and dun wreathes of smoke curling and streaming across the face of heaven, the smoke of bursting explosives sent from earth to cripple the fliers in mid-air.

Gazing on the battle struggle with all its empty passion and deadly hatred, I thought of the worshipper of old who looked on the face of God, and, seeing His face, died. And the scene before me, like the Countenance of the Creator, was not good for mortal eye.

He who has known and felt the romance of the long night marches can never forget it. The departure from barn billets when the blue evening sky fades into palest saffron, and the drowsy ringing of church bells in the neighbouring village calling the worshippers to evensong; the singing of the men who swing away, accoutred in the harness of war; the lights of little white houses beaming into the darkness; the stars stealing silently out in the hazy bowl of the sky; the trees by the roadside standing stiff and stark in the twilight as if listening and waiting for something to take place; the soft, warm night, half moonlight and half mist, settling over mining villages with their chimneys, railways, signal lights, slag-heaps, rattling engines and dusty trucks.

There is a quicker throbbing of the heart when the men arrive at the crest of the hill, well known to all, but presenting fresh aspects every time the soldier reaches its summit, that overlooks the firing line.

Ahead, the star-shells, constellations of green, electric white, and blue, light the scenes of war. From the ridge of the hill, downwards towards an illimitable plain, the road takes its way through a ghost-world of ruined homes where dark and ragged masses of broken roof and wall stand out in blurred outlines against indistinct and formless backgrounds.

A gun is belching forth murder and sudden

death from an emplacement on the right; in a spinney on the left a battery is noisy and the flashes from there light up the cluster of trees that stand huddled together as if for warmth. Vehicles of war lumber along the road, field-kitchens, gun-limbers, water-carts, motor-ambulances, and Red Cross waggons. Men march towards us, men in brown, bearing rifles and swords, and pass us in the night. A shell bursts near, and there is a sound as of a handful of peas being violently flung to the ground.

For the night we stop in a village where the branches of the trees are shrapnelled clean of their leaves, and where all the rafters of the houses are bared of their covering of red tiles. A wind may rise when you're dropping off to sleep on the stone flags of a cellar, and then you can hear the door of the house and of nearly every house in the place creaking on its hinges. The breeze catches the telephone wires which run from the artillery at rear to their observation stations, and the wires sing like light shells travelling through space.

At dawn you waken to the sound of anti-aircraft guns firing at aeroplanes which they never bring down. The bullets, falling back from exploding shells, swish to the earth with a sound like burning magnesium wires and split a tile if any is left, or crack a skull, if any is in the way, with the neatest dispatch. It is wise to remain in shelter until the row is over.

Outside, the birds are merry on the roofs; you can hear them sing defiantly at the lone cat that watches them from the grassy spot which was once a street. Spiders' webs hang over the doorways, many flies have come to an untimely end in the glistening snares, poor little black, helpless things. Here and there lies a broken crucifix and a torn picture of the Holy Family, the shrines that once stood at the street corners are shapeless heaps of dust and weeds and the village church is in ruins.

No man is allowed to walk in the open by day; a German observation balloon, a big banana of a thing, with ends pointing downwards stands high over the earth ten kilometres away and sees all that takes place in the streets.

There is a soldiers' cemetery to rear of the last block of buildings where the dead have been shovelled out of earth by shell fire. In this village the dead are out in the open whilst the quick are underground.

How fine it is to leave the trenches at night

after days of innumerable fatigues and make for a hamlet, well back, where beer is good and where soups and salads are excellent. When the feet are sore and swollen, and when the pack-straps cut the shoulder like a knife, the journey may be tiring, but the glorious rest in a musty old barn, with creaking stairs and cobwebbed rafters, amply compensates for all the strain of getting there.

Lazily we drop into the straw, loosen our puttees and shoes and light a soothing cigarette from our little candles. The whole barn is a chamber of mysterious light and shade and strange rustlings. The flames of the candles dance on the walls, the stars peep through the roof. Eyes, strangely brilliant under the shadow of the brows, meet one another inquiringly.

"Is this not a night?" they seem to ask. "The night of all the world?"

Apart from that, everybody is quiet, we lie still resting, resting. Probably we shall fall asleep as we drop down, only to wake again when the cigarettes burn to the fingers. We can take full advantage of a rest, as a rest is known to the gloriously weary.

There is romance, there is joy in the life of a soldier.

THE END.